Beyond Belief

Edited by **RICHARD J. HURLEY**

Cover by **DENNY McMAINS**

SCHOLASTIC BOOK SERVICES
NEW YORK • TORONTO • LONDON • AUCKLAND • SYDNEY • TOKYO

CONTENTS

Dedicated to all my fellow Terrans, young in heart and spirit whether six or sixty, and especially to my neighbor and friend Phil Dresser.

The Hardest Bargain

by *Evelyn E. Smith*

T HERE IS a group of citizens engaged in rioting
on the lawn, sir," Robot Z-1313A told the
President of the United States. "Trampling down
the early peas, too," he added, with the objective
interest of one whose chief article of diet was oil.

"Well, don't just stand there," President Buchbinder said. "Go out and chase them away!" His
voice subsided to a groan. "Have the people no
respect for our sacred traditions? Don't they know
the White House lawn is the only place for miles
around where peas will grow?"

"They're young, most of them," Dr. Livingston,
the President's confidential adviser, said toler-
antly, puffing at his pipe. "The way the birth rate's
been climbing, you take any given number of
the population at any one time and the majority

1

will be too young to remember our glorious traditions. . . ."

"Their parents could teach them!" Buchbinder snapped. "After all, isn't that why we have parents instead of incubators?"

"Their parents are too busy scratching out a living and — ah — breeding to be able to instruct the young ones," Livingston said. "It's a vicious circle which has come to a head in this generation."

There was something wrong with that statement, Buchbinder knew, but he didn't dare come right out and say so, for fear of looking a fool. He knew his confidential adviser was smarter than he was. And what with the atomic wars of the past couple of centuries, the large proportion of strontium 90 in the atmosphere, and general intellectual jealousy, there weren't many intelligent people left in the world, so the ones that remained had to be handled with care.

Buchbinder turned to Z-1313A, who was still standing there. "Why haven't you obeyed my instructions?" he demanded, outraged at this evidence of insubordination in a robot. From people you expected it, but a machine was supposed to be above such petty defectiveness. "Why don't you go chase the rioters off the lawn, per order?"

"I don't dare, sir," Z-1313A explained. "Should I get close enough, they would disassemble me. As a matter of fact, when I informed them from the balcony that they were trespassing, they employed language which — well, sir, if I hadn't been a robot and constitutionally incapable of the prudent graces, it would have made me blush."

"Disassemble a robot!" Buchbinder repeated, shocked. "I never heard of anything so manic in my life. Why should they want to do a thing like that?"

Since the robot did not have parts sufficiently flexible for shrugging, he remained impassive. It was Dr. Livingston who answered. "Haven't you heard, Will? The people are starting to destroy robots when they can get their hands on them. To try to destroy them, that is. Fortunately, most of the people are too weak from hunger and racial debility to do any great damage unless they operate in gangs. Looks like you'll have to pass an anticongregation law."

"But why should they want to do a silly thing like destroying robots?" Buchbinder persisted.

Livingston smiled wisely. "They're saying that if it weren't for the robots, they'd have jobs, a higher standard of living — the usual complaints you hear at the beginning of every revolution."

"If it weren't for the robots, they wouldn't have anything at all!" Buchbinder said, exasperated. "Don't they realize that the only thing that keeps the country going at all is the fact that there's a plentiful supply of free labor? And I understand from Counterintelligence that it's the same overseas."

"Oh, there's plenty of free labor," Livingston observed. "Plenty of service, too. But very little to eat."

"That's not true," Buchbinder said hotly. "Maybe hydroponics didn't work out for large-scale operations; still, the people could perfectly well eat synthetics. But, no, they're so stubborn, they'd rather starve to death."

"Some of them did eat the synthetics and died anyway."

"Some people insist on being allergic to anything! It's all in the mind!" At times like this, Buchbinder felt he was on the verge of going mad, like Presidents Ling and Riccobono before him. If only he had been elected in the days before the atomic wars, when it was a treat to be President! Then, all a Chief Executive had to do were fun things, like appointing ambassadors and making speeches and declaring wars. He didn't have to worry how to feed the people; in those days, there used to be food growing all over the place and it was distributed with such efficiency that only a small portion of the populace ever went hungry.

"You'd think since they know there isn't much food," Buchbinder said, "that people wouldn't have quite so many children and make more mouths to feed."

"I don't suppose they're doing it consciously," Livingston told him. "It's nature's attempt to ensure the survival of the race. And it certainly looks from here as if it's likely to be a futile one."

"You're always so pessimistic, Maurice."

Dr. Livingston cleared his throat, as he always did before making a remark he felt to be especially apt. "The thinking man," he said, "is the despairing man."

Robot Z-1313B came into the President's office. "A ship from outer space has landed on the lawn, sir," he announced, "thus, I am sure you will be gratified to know, effectively disposing of the rioters."

"Oh, good!" Robot Z-1313A said. "That disposes of my problem."

Both robots shook hands with a slight grating noise.

"But if there were any peas left," Buchbinder mourned, "this must have finished them."

However, he arose, for when duty summoned, Willis Buchbinder, though possibly reluctant, was never remiss.

"I don't see why the star traders keep on coming all the way out here," he remarked as he put on the sacred frock coat with the authentic moth holes. "Surely what little we have to trade wouldn't be of much value to them."

Livingston took his pipe out of his mouth. "I

imagine there must always be little novelty items they can pick up. After all, the fact that we're so far off the beaten track probably gives our products some curio value, if nothing else."

"Oh, I suppose so," Buchbinder sighed. "All right, activate the reception committee," he told Z-1313B. "I don't suppose there's any chance this could be a diplomatic mission or anything like that?" he added wistfully, brushing off the tall genuine silk ceremonial hat.

"No, sir, it is merely a trading ship — and rather a small one," said Z-1313B, who left to turn on the reception committee. That was merely a fancy name for a unitranslator which the government had purchased from a Denebian trader some decades before in return for a partridge in a pear tree. The bargain had, of course, been closed in the days when neither partridges nor pear trees had become obsolescent.

Although interstellar traders had been dropping in on Earth for the past hundred years or so, Earth had no diplomatic relations with the other solar systems — or any kind of official relations at all, in fact. As far as the terrestrials could make out from the information given them by the various life forms which hit Earth from time to time those days, there had been some kind of embargo on their planet for many centuries. If the more extravagant reports were to be believed, the sanctions dated back to the time when there were no powered vehicles on Earth.

At any rate, as a result of these discriminatory tactics, Earth citizens were not allowed to ride in the extraterrestrial ships back to their point of origin. It was very likely that an attempt would have been made to prevent them from traveling in their own ships, if they'd had any. Fortunately, however, Earth had not succeeded in developing space travel and so the question never arose.

"Used to be an embargo on all trade, even," a chatty Aldebaranian octopoid had told President Ling. "Now the league seems to be easing up a little on nonvital materials. Who knows, maybe someday when you're advanced enough or something, they'll even let you into the League. . . . Now what do you have to offer in fine glass and crystal?"

"If we didn't need food," Buchbinder declared, "I wouldn't speak to one of those outworlders. If we're not good enough for them, I don't see why . . ."

"But we do need food," Livingston said, taking his pipe out of his mouth and pointing it at the President. "Desperately. You have no choice but to dicker with him."

Buchbinder nodded gloomily.

"On the other hand, Will, do you think it dignified to go drive the bargain yourself? What do you have a Secretary of the Interior for?"

"St. Clair?" Buchbinder cried contemptuously. "Why, I wouldn't trust him as far as I could spit. Less, in fact, because I used to be the champion . . ."

"Willis, Willis," Livingston chided gently as he, too, pulled on his frock coat, "this is no time for dithering."

"If that St. Clair saw a chance to make a fast buck for himself," Buchbinder grumbled, "he wouldn't care about the country. Besides, if there happen to be any truffles, I want to put my bid in for them first. The last time, Defense got them all. And when I reminded General McMullen that, after all, I was Commander in Chief, he said he was sorry, but the top brass had already eaten them all in a souffle.

"Have you ever thought, Maurice," Buchbinder continued as, fully attired in the traditional ceremonial garments, the two dignitaries clattered down the grand stairs, "how funny it is that these extraterrestrial fellows should have the exact kind of food we eat? I mean it's obvious that they're completely different life forms with different digestive systems and everything. Some aren't even animals and yet they bring — well, oats, peas, beans, and barley. Earth food."

"It's obvious they must know a great deal about

us," Livingston answered. "We *are* worth a bit of study. So it's not hard to understand . . ."

"I'm not asking how they know what we eat," Buchbinder said. "I'm asking where they get it from. And all properly put up in cans, too."

"It doesn't take a great deal of know-how to put up food in cans. Posnack's experiments with chimpanzees conclusively . . ."

"I didn't mean . . ." Buchbinder interrupted. Then he forgot what he was starting to say as he tripped over a roller skate on the bottom step. "Even here," he said bitterly. "In the White House. Children."

"Must be the Secretary of Agriculture's twins," Livingston said. "He brings them to work to save the cost of a baby-sitter."

The reception committee proved to be unnecessary; the trader spoke fluent English. He was also vaguely humanoid, being a biped with only one pair of arms and one rather small head. It was in skin-coloring that the difference between him and the human was most marked, not so much in hue as in arrangement, for his complexion ranged from the ruddy bronze of the American Indian on one side of his scantily clothed body to a Mongolian ochre on the other. Had he been portly rather than thin, he would have resembled an apple. His name was Foma and he came from the Fomalhaut system.

Foma was one of the most attractive outworlders Buchbinder had ever seen, although the President's favorable opinion was undoubtedly influenced by the fact that the alien had not only brought cans of truffles but sauerkraut and pâté de fois gras and beer as well. There were herrings and jam and jellybeans put up in clear, shining glass jars, and lovely plump knockwursts and Brunschweiger sausages neatly encased in their own skins. He had plastic bags of pretzels and potatoes, and his frozen-food locker actually contained stewed rabbit and pumpernickel and three kinds of strudel.

Foma drove a hard bargain, for he wanted a considerable quantity of Revere silver in return for all these delightful things. However, Buchbinder was no slouch at haggling, either, and he managed to beat down the alien two teapots and a creamer before the bargain was closed.

Then the robots swiftly carried the crates of food into the White House, where a certain portion would be reserved for the government tables. The rest would be carried by other robots to Fort Knox, from which it would be dispensed to the general population according to merit, rank, and connections. And, as the food was taken out of the ship, the crowd of children outside the fence, who had been emitting shrill jeers and cat-calls throughout the preliminary parleying, fell silent and reverent before the almost legendary dainties borne past them.

"Nice little machines you have there," Foma said, surveying the robots appreciatively. "Is there any chance that you would consider parting with some? I'll give you a good price."

"Oh, no, decidedly not!" the President exclaimed, horrified at such a suggestion. "These were the last creations of our greatest minds before they died," he explained, "and our economy, such as it is, was founded upon them. We couldn't do without our robots. And there's an arbitrary limit on their numbers built in as one of the prime directives. They manufacture themselves, you see," he went on, anxious not to offend the outworlder, "which is why we have none available for export."

"I do see," Foma said with a smile. "What I can't understand, though, is how you people managed to survive with an economy based on food that doesn't seem to be indigenous to your planet."

"Oh, but it used to be," the President replied wistfully.

He made a sweeping gesture that embraced all of the District of Columbia and part of Maryland. "Once, verdant vegetation stretched as far as the eye could see, while edible animals gamboled about blissfully in it. Why," he cried, carried away, "prior to the twenty-first century, the whole country looked like a combined zoological and botanical garden."

"It must have been very pretty," Foma said.

"Not that it isn't pretty now," he added with polite haste. "A very pleasant spot. A river does so much for a town, and that's a very charming river washing the southern side—"

"The western side," Livingston corrected him thoughtfully. "If you mean the Potomac."

"The southwestern side, to be exact," the President said, exercising diplomacy. "However, you should have seen the place before the wars. I understand it was a veritable fairyland!" He grew sad. "But then came the wars. Most of the land was devastated by those terrible nuclear weapons, except for small patches here and there left fertile by chance. The scientists say nothing will grow on most of it for hundreds of years, by which time the race will have died out, I suppose." He gave a brave smile. "Ah, well, it was fun while it lasted."

"I don't mean to presume," Foma said, "but I suppose you could derive a little moral lesson from what happened: to wit, fighting is unprofitable as well as unethical."

"Oh, the human being has always been a fighting animal," Dr. Livingston replied. "If you must have a moral, it might be—" he cleared his throat — "if your weapons are too good, you'll kill off all the game."

Foma gave the confidential adviser a chilling stare, then turned back to Buchbinder. "I am beginning to understand now why you don't rehabilitate your land and start growing things again. I had wondered, but I see now you realize that the same thing would only happen all over again, so it's no use. I really admire you, though, for your national strength of character in . . ."

"Rehabilitate the land?" Buchbinder repeated incredulously. "You mean the radioactivity can be removed from the soil?"

"Hasn't anyone ever told you?" Foma asked. "Wait a minute, though," he added consideringly. "I might be treading on classified ground. I must consult my handbook."

Placing what looked like a species of optical instrument before his face, he twirled several knobs.

"No," he announced as he removed it, "not classified at all. I'm forced to the shocking conclusion that the other traders didn't want to dry up a profitable source of revenue by decontaminating your land."

"Well, even if such a process were possible," Livingston said, "you can hardly blame them. After all, business is business."

Foma looked at him sternly.

These philosophical irrelevancies made the President impatient. "Do you mean you have a way of removing the radioactivity . . . ?"

"Watch out," Livingston whispered. "This looks like the beginning of a sharp practice to me. Personally, I don't believe there is any such process."

Apparently the outworlder's hearing was more acute than the human. "You Earth people are so suspicious. No wonder . . ." And then he stopped.

"No wonder what?" Livingston pressed.

"Just no wonder," Foma said firmly. He turned to the President. "Would you like your land decontaminated? By good fortune, I do happen to have the requisite equipment for taking the radioactivity out of soil. The same machine is used for many things."

"Aha!" Dr. Livingston cried. "Good fortune, indeed!" He cleared his throat. "The coincidence in the natural state is an extremely rare bird."

"I'm not denying that it is rather an expensive process," Foma continued, ignoring him. "But when you need something done, you've got to pay — the price."

It was pretty depressing, Buchbinder thought, to know that there was a cure for your ailment and not have the money to pay for the medicine.

"We have so little," he said hopelessly. "So very little. What can we offer that will make it worth your while?"

"You underestimate the value of your native handicrafts," Foma smiled. "I will undertake to remove the radioactivity from the entire country," he offered, changing to a brisk, businesslike tone, "in return for the following . . ." Putting his optical instrument to his eye again, he read aloud: "Rembrandt, *Old Woman Cutting Her*

Nails; El Greco, *View of Toledo;* Titian, *Venus and Adonis;* Daumier, *Third-class Carriage;* Goya, *Don Manuel Osorio;* Cézanne, *Card Players;* and Picasso, *The Three Musicians.*"

"What's all that in English?" Buchbinder asked, thinking that Foma, in his enthusiasm, had lapsed into his native tongue. "Are you sure we have it?"

"He was speaking English," Livingston hissed. "Those are pictures, famous paintings. Among the nation's most treasured artistic possessions. We can hardly sell them for —" he gave a bitter little laugh — "food."

"You mean better we should starve than sell them?" Buchbinder asked.

"Better we should starve," Livingston said solemnly.

The President struggled hard to understand. "But we sold him the teapots and they're historical. They were made by Paul Revere and he . . ."

"I know all about Paul Revere, thank you," Livingston said.

"And these are just pictures. From the way they sounded, they were all painted by foreigners. And Paul Revere was an American. A patriot—"

"I know, I know," Livingston interrupted. "On the twenty-second of July in 'seventy-six . . ."

"Now even I know better than that," Buchbinder said, staring at him in amazement, as did the alien. "It's 'On the eighteenth of April in 'seventy-five . . .'"

"Of course," Livingston murmured. "Now why did my subconscious make me get the date wrong like that?"

"Human memory is fallible," Foma suggested suavely.

The President tugged insistently at Livingston's sleeve. "You're willing to sell the teapots of this great American patriot, but when it comes to things that were made by foreigners . . ."

"You simply don't understand, Willis."

"I know I don't." Buchbinder's voice was plaintive. "That's why I'm asking you to explain to me."

"Paul Revere was a great man and a fine silversmith. It is a pity to let his creations go out of our solar system. However —" Livingston cleared his throat — "purely utilitarian objects never attain the artistic dignity of beauty created for its own sake."

"Why?" the President wanted to know.

Livingston gave a sigh and turned to the outworlder. "Look, Mr. — ah — Foma, I'm afraid it will require a special session of Congress to settle this matter. Would you mind waiting a few weeks? Or months?"

"Or, possibly, years," the President grumbled.

"Not at all," Foma said smiling. "I shall amuse

myself by browsing through the Congressional Library. Perhaps I can locate one or two little items there that we can make a deal on."

Both houses of Congress tended to support the President's point of view. "For," the Senate majority leader orated, "splendid and enduring monuments to our nation's greatness though these works of art may be . . ."

"They weren't even painted by Americans," Buchbinder interposed helpfully.

The majority leader glared at him. "I didn't say they *were* splendid and enduring monuments to our nation's greatness. I only said they *may* be. Anyhow, should the race perish, there will be no one to look at these beautiful pictures and appreciate their — er — beauty. But then again, should we entrust them to the keeping of the gentleman from the stars?" he bowed toward Foma. "I am sure that his people will preserve them with the same loving care and solicitude that we ourselves have given them."

"You may rest assured of that," Foma promised, returning the bow.

"Then, when our lands are fruitful once more, when we are able to give of their abundance to our four-footed friends, so that the animal kingdom may thrive and multiply again, when our race has regained its former glory, invigorated by the renewal of plenty and a reliable supply of meat, we shall develop space travel of our own. A mighty fleet shall set sail for the stars—"

"Hear, hear!" shrieked the children who filled the gallery to bursting.

"— we shall seek out the strongholds where the pictures are kept," the Senator continued, "and then we—" he glanced at Foma and seemed to recollect himself— "and then we will look at them."

There were boos and catcalls from the gallery.

"Silence!" bellowed the Congressional robots. "Si-lence!"

"But who's to say this alleged process will work?" the minority leader asked. President Buchbinder knew he was a close associate of Dr. Livingston's. "Mr. Foma may make off with our paintings and leave the land as barren as ever."

"Naturally, I shall not ask for payment, gentlemen," Foma said, "until your lands are green once more."

"Well," the minority leader concluded lamely, "nothing can be fairer than that. I guess."

That seemed to settle it. Congress passed an act empowering the alien to commence rehabilitating the barren lands. Dr. Livingston remained in Washington to keep the eternal light burning over the tombs of the numerous Unknown Soldiers, while Foma and President Buchbinder set off for Smith County, Kansas. Smith County, Kansas, was the geographical center of the United

States and hence the place where Foma proposed to set up his equipment.

"Doesn't seem like much," Buchbinder observed as Foma, with the efficient aid of some of the Smith County robots, put together a simple contraption of wheels, springs, pipes, valves, relays, switches, coils, shafts, and wires.

"Perhaps not," Foma said affably, "but it is highly effective. When activated, the machine disseminates powerful sonic rays which will accelerate the diminution of the halflife of the soil until, in very short order, it becomes only a quarterlife, then an eighthlife, a sixteenthlife —"

"I understand," the President interrupted. "But how long does it take until there is no life at all — no radioactive life, that is?"

"Perhaps a week," Foma said. "Perhaps eight days, perhaps six."

"I'd also like to know," the President inquired apprehensively buttoning his jacket up to his throat, "whether it does anything to people. Because it's not much good if the soil turns fertile and we turn the opposite."

"At this setting," Foma said, "it has not the slightest effect upon any form of animal life."

He beamed upon the Smith County children who had gathered to watch the proceedings. They stuck out their tongues at him. Buchbinder hoped that wherever the alien came from, it was a gesture of great respect.

Then the President had a frightening thought. "The emanations won't reach the Eastern Empire, will they? We wouldn't want their soil to become fertile again."

"You are paying to have this country decontaminated," Foma said, "and only this country will be decontaminated. I do not offer my services gratis. People set no value on anything for which they do not pay."

"Well, of course not!" President Buchbinder agreed. Then he had an even more appalling idea. The Eastern Empire, he'd been given to understand, had some art treasures of its own in a place called the Hermitage. "After you've finished with us," he asked, "you're not going to turn around and make a deal with the East to decontaminate them, are you?"

"That," Foma said curtly as he blew into one of the pipes, "is my business."

"Oh, dear," the President thought, "it is going to mean more wars. Well," he consoled himself, "war is more interesting than riots and, as a matter of fact, a lot safer for me personally, since rioters always make for the White House first, whereas war is on a more catch-as-catch-can basis."

At the end of the week, Foma reported that the machine's work was done and dismantled it. President Buchbinder was thankful, for the sonic vibrations were nerve-wracking and people had

been complaining, even though he had made a
video address to the nation beforehand to explain
just what they were supposed to do. Now he made
another address, exhorting everyone who had any
ground at all to go forth and plant seeds.

"And in case the seeds we have should not
prove viable," he concluded, "Mr. Foma has been
kind enought to throw a group of vegetable seeds
from his own stock into the bargain. Do not
think, however," he reassured the nation, "that
these are the seeds of alien vegetation. On the
contrary, we have Swiss chard, cabbage, beets,
onions, cucumbers, Brussels sprouts, and rhubarb
— all perfectly familiar — I may even say beloved
— native vegetables."

As they went off the air, the President remembered a question that had been bothering him
earlier.

"You don't look like us," he said to Foma. "How
come you grow exactly the same vegetables as we
used to?"

"A trader must have brought some seeds back
from this planet," Foma said. "Must have been a
long time ago, too, because the vegetables you
describe as yours flourish on a good many of the
other worlds now. Although we don't care for the
produce ourselves, some of our pets like them,
which is why we happened to have supplies on
hand when we reopened trading operations with
you."

"Oh," the President said. It sounded reasonable enough.

After the broadcast, Foma and President Buchbinder returned to Washington, where Foma reveled in the pleasures of the Congressional Library and the Folger Memorial for some weeks. Then the seeds, both local and imported, began to sprout and the land turned green, according to promise, and Foma's bill came due.

"Mr. Foma of Fomalhaut to see you," Robot X-1313B announced as he came into the President's office, where Buchbinder and Livingston were playing chess.

"Sorry I couldn't wait to have an appointment put through the regular channels," Foma said, coming in hard upon the robot's heels.

"Oh, my dear fellow," said Buchbinder, rising, "think nothing of it — we are very informal here. What can I do for you?"

"Now that my part of the bargain is fulfilled, I'm rather anxious to go home, so I'd appreciate immediate payment of my bill."

"Of course, of course! I'll start getting the pictures together. You should have them by the end of the week."

"Excellent." The alien smiled. "Meanwhile, I'll get my ship ready for the return journey." He shook hands with Buchbinder and left.

"You won't have to bother getting the pictures together," Dr. Livingston said as soon as Foma had gone. "They're all in the basement already."

"Maurice," the President said feelingly, "you did this for me while I was gone. You put aside your personal prejudices in order to save me trouble. You . . ."

"Well," Livingston interrupted uncomfortably, "you might as well know now: they're not exactly the same pictures he asked for. While you were gone, I got together with a little Congressional committee and we decided . . ."

"But we promised!" Buchbinder exclaimed in dismay. "We agreed on seven specific pictures. They're listed right here on the bill he rendered!"

"We didn't sign a contract," Livingston said, pushing away the paper the President was thrusting in his face. "Besides, he *is* getting pictures. Masterpieces, too. But more the kind his people will be able to appreciate."

"How do you know that?"

"Look, I'll show them to you."

Dr. Livingston led the President down to the basement. "Here's what Foma's getting," he explained. "Instead of Rembrandt's *Old Woman Cutting Her Nails*, we give him Delacroix's *Arab Tax Collector*. Instead of El Greco's *View of Toledo*, he gets Constable's *Wivenhoe Park, Essex*. For Titian's *Venus and Adonis,* Hals' *Junker Ramp and His Sweetheart*. For Daumier's *Third-class Carriage*, Eastman's *My Old Kentucky Home*. For Goya's *Don Manuel Osorio,* Canaletto's *Vege-*

table Garden. For Cézanne's *Card Players,* Fragonard's *A Game of Hot Cockles.* And for Picasso's *The Three Musicians,* Murillo's *Jacob and Rachel at the Well.*"

"Yes, they are very pretty pictures," the President said, inspecting them. "Very pretty, indeed. I can see how we'd hate to let them go."

"No, no, no!" Livingston cried. "These are the ones we're giving him! Nothing but the best, you see. And, on the average, much larger than the ones he asked for. Why, he might not even have known about these; they are less publicized, so outworlders might not have heard of them."

"That's very considerate of you, Maurice," the President said, "but since we are giving him masterpieces, anyway, why don't we let him have the ones he asked for? Why go to all this trouble?"

"I'll tell you, Will," said Livingston. "It's because the nation has more of a sentimental attachment to the others. And, furthermore, the pictures we are giving him present a more favorable view of terrestrial life. The others — well, I hate to say it about masterpieces, Willis, but some of them might almost be considered sordid. And one of these was painted by an American."

"These *are* nice." The President didn't know much about art, but he didn't see how anybody could help liking the pictures Livingston and the Congressional committee had selected. "*Very* nice."

"That's just it, Will!" Livingston clapped him on the shoulder. "You've hit it exactly. They're *nice!* They're the kind of pictures we'd be proud to have another world see. We want to make a good impression in the other solar systems, don't we, so someday maybe we can get into the Big League ourselves?"

He was convincing, but Buchbinder was still dubious. "Are you sure Foma will understand? He might make a fuss. And he has every right to, you know."

"We'll get the robots to do these up in special gift-wrapping paper," Livingston said, "with ribbons and seals and all, and maybe Foma won't open them until he gets to his home planet."

"Maybe," the President half agreed. "But even if he doesn't open them, somehow it doesn't seem right. Maurice, don't you think we're going to sacrifice a lot of interstellar good will if we pull a trick like this?"

"Nonsense! It's just sound business practice." Livingston cleared his throat. "Besides, we cannot let mere material considerations interfere with our duty."

"I suppose not," the President said. "On the other hand . . ."

"I'll call the robots and have them start wrapping right away," Livingston told him.

"But these aren't the pictures Mr. Foma asked for," Z-1313A said helpfully as he brought out the big roll of gold-foil gift-wrapping paper, with "Compliments of the White House," "Regards from the President," and "Best Wishes from the U.S.A." etched on it in flowing script. "Someone apparently has blundered. Shall we . . ."

"There's no mistake," the President said, the more impatiently as he could not, in spite of Dr. Livingston's assurances, get his conscience to accept this switching of art works.

"They don't look to me like pictures anybody would ask for," Z-1313B contributed.

"They're not supposed to appeal to *mechanical* tastes!" Buchbinder snapped. "I like them."

"Use the seals that say 'Do Not Open until Inauguration Day,'" Livingston told the robots, "and the heaviest wrapping tape. And be sure you make the knots good and tight, but very ornate, so it'll seem a pity to undo them."

When the pictures were all wrapped, the robots carried them out carefully to the lawn. Foma was waiting next to his ship, in the midst of a welter of debris left by the children who had come to look at it while he was gone. Its once shining metallic sides were marred by scratches and even paint. Some of the disfiguring marks were words.

Buchbinder spelled them out laboriously: "MONSSTER GO HOAM!" "PREZIDENT BUK-BINDER LOVS EXTERATERESTRIALS!" "DR LIVINSTUN ISNT AS SMART AS HE THINX HE IS!"

"Oh, my goodness!" the President exclaimed. "What a dreadful thing to have happen! I'll have the robots clean it up at once!"

"Children will be children," Foma smiled. "I find the slogans rather amusing and, in fact, almost decorative. I won't have them touched." And he started to turn to the pictures.

The President gave a scared little gasp. "You've forgotten something!" he babbled. "Under the tarpaulin. Maybe it's important!" He started to lift the tarpaulin, but Foma stopped him.

"No, I haven't forgotten that. It's — ah — some gear that can't be put on board until after the cargo is loaded. Would you take the paper off the pictures?" he said to the robots.

"They did them up so nicely," the President said in a small voice. "It — it seems such a shame —"

"Don't worry about it," Foma told him. "I'm going to put them away in special hyperspace-proof batting, anyhow. And I wouldn't be much of a trader if I bought goods sight unseen, now would I?"

The three of them stood there in a dead silence as the robots unwrapped each picture.

Foma's eyes chilled into steel, including the one which had opened in the middle of his forehead. "These are not the pictures I asked for."

"These are fine pictures," Buchbinder faltered. "Very fine —"

"They are very fine pictures. However, our bargain was for seven others. I kept my part of the bargain; I expect you to keep yours."

Livingston shrugged. "I'm afraid you hardly have much choice. You can't contaminate the country all over again. Even if you have the means to do it, I feel sure that your League would consider such behavior unethical."

"You're quite right," Foma agreed, "although I am rather surprised to find you able to even recognize an ethical point of view."

Livingston grasped the alien's arm. "Be reasonable, man — er — Mr. Foma. These are excellent pictures we're offering you, in tiptop condition. Only the best of pigments — and have you ever seen handsomer frames?"

Foma shook him off. "Those are not the pictures we agreed upon. I refuse to accept them in payment of your debt."

Livingston grinned. "If you persist in your obstinacy, sir, I'm afraid you'll have to go back to your planet unpaid."

"Maurice, Maurice," the President whimpered, tugging at his adviser's sleeve, "this will give us a bad name in the Galaxy. They won't come with food to trade any more."

"We won't need their food, lunkhead!" Livingston snapped. "We can grow our own now." He turned back to Foma. "That's our final offer, sir. Take it or leave it!"

"Your final offer, eh?" Foma repeated. "Very well, then."

"Maurice," Buchbinder bleated, "I'm afraid . . ."

"Shut up, Willis!"

Foma yanked the tarpaulin away and disclosed what had been concealed underneath it—his decontamination apparatus, already set up.

"You're going to make the land radioactive again!" the President gasped. "I told you, Maurice . . ."

"He wouldn't dare!" Dr. Livingston cried, but he was pale.

"No," Foma said, "I shall do nothing of the sort. All I want are my just dues. And, as I told you, this is an extremely versatile machine." He blew into a pipe.

There was a moment of silence — a moment in which nothing happened, but everything seemed about to happen. Then there was a clattering sound. And all of a sudden, the streets were filled with robots. They streamed down Pennsylvania Avenue, they streamed down Connecticut Avenue, marching in perfect unison.

They marched toward the White House; they marched onto the lawn; they marched up the ramp and into the airlock of the spaceship, which expanded in a seemingly limitless way to accommodate them.

Hundreds of them came, stolidly marching; thousands came, tens of thousands . . . until it was clear that the District of Columbia and its surrounding communities were being drained of their robots.

"Call out the Army!" shouted the President. "Call out the Navy! Summon the Marine Corps!"

"They're all robots," Livingston said in a tired voice. "Except for the officers, of course, and all they can do is head parades and initial computer directives."

"The Secret Service? . . . No," the President answered himself. "If the soldiers and sailors and marines are robots, then the Secret Service certainly must be." He appealed to Foma. "Please turn off the machine! Turn it off! I'll get you the pictures you wanted — and you can have these into the bargain. You can have the whole National Gallery, only please don't take our robots!"

"Too late," said Foma, and his voice was grand and sad and smug. "Too late. A deal is a deal. When it's broken, the injured party has every right to exact whatever payment he deems fit."

Dr. Livingston stared at Foma, his eyes widening, then widening still further. "Then it *wasn't* a legend! You actually did it."

Foma bowed low.

"What are you two agreeing about?" the President asked, looking bewilderedly from one to the other.

Dr. Livingston ignored him. "Then take the children! Leave us our robots!"

"We took the children a thousand years ago," said Foma, "in payment for another bad debt, using an earlier model of this same machine. But that was only because there was nothing better to take. We also hoped — naively, as it turned out — that the lesson would teach you the high cost of sharp practice."

"Oh, I remember!" the President exclaimed. "You got rid of the rats in some foreign town. And then, when the town officials wouldn't pay up, you took the children. Some fellow wrote a poem about it — a rather long one that we studied in school. . . . That must be how come you got the dates mixed up, Maurice," he added, pleased with his own deductive faculties.

"We took a considerable loss on that deal," Foma said, "because we found that, though human children make delightful pets, they're not much good when they grow up — absolutely no talent for solid, honest labor. No, the robots we can use; the children you can keep."

Dr. Livingston cleared his throat, uncomfortably this time, not complacently. "Then there really is an embargo on us."

"Yes, it was placed upon Earth on July 22, 1376, at a little town in Germany called Hameln — or, as Browning misspelled it — Hamelin. In fact, that swindle is what gave rise to a simile we have in the Galaxy: 'As untrustworthy as an Earthman.' Obviously we cannot have diplomatic relations with a species that fits the slogan so exactly, especially after this piece of trickery. The embargo still stands."

The airlock clanged to and whirled shut behind him.

Buchbinder and Livingston watched disconsolately as the spaceship zoomed up into the stratosphere.

"Now we'll never make the Big League," the President moaned.

"Aah, what kind of League would send a piper out as an emissary?" sneered Livingston. "And a pied piper, to boot."

And so the alien vessel hurtled out into space, taking all the robots in the country with it, except for a poor little crippled model from the West Coast, whose reaction time was as defective as his judgment. He arrived from California two weeks later and was so upset at finding himself left behind that he fused completely.

Unrepresentative though he was of the strong handsome, efficient robots that had gone with Foma, he was all the nation had to memorialize those it had once proudly owned, and he was given a niche in the Hall of Fame. He has the largest bronze plaque there — Browning's poem, engraved all around the base — with appropriate footnotes by historians.

The Invasion

by Robert Willey

To tens of millions of television viewers and to the only slightly smaller number who have attended his lectures, the face and lingeringly Germanic tones of Willy Ley are familiar in the role of The Man Who Explains Science . . . a part which nature and training have beautifully equipped him to play. In the old pre-Hitler Germany, Willy Ley was an associate of the early rocket experimenters, whose work led directly to Peenemünde — and ultimately to space.

The universe of science fiction readers knows Willy Ley too — for his many articles in all science fiction magazines over a twenty-year period, for his regular column in every issue of Galaxy Magazine and also (as "Robert Willey") for a

*few, but qualitatively memorable, stories of which
"The Invasion" is only one example.*

W<small>ALTER</small> H<small>ARLING</small> watched the soldiers as they
fed a clip of long and dangerous looking car-
tridges into the magazine of the antiaircraft gun.
The thin, multiple barrels pointed almost verti-
cally into the air and toward the foliage of large
and beautiful trees that hid them from sight of
enemy aircraft. At their muzzles these long barrels carried clumsy-looking drumlike contrap-
tions, Schneider recoil brakes that diverted the
flow of the gases resulting from the explosion of
the cartridges in such a way that counter-recoil
balanced original recoil and held the guns steady.

Tightly fitting rubber-lined metal lids covered
the outer muzzles of the recoil brakes. Rain water
must not flow into the barrel else nobody could
guarantee what would happen if the guns were to
be used suddenly. It was raining hard, as it had
rained for many hours. And although it was not
even late in the afternoon, it was almost completely dark. One could just distinguish the nearest
trees and the guns in the damp, dark air.

The battery was in position not far from the
road. On the other side of it, on a clearing that
had been a famous camping ground in this forest
— one of the nation's most beautiful national for-

ests — stood a battery of eight-inch howitzers. They were firing rhythmically. Walter Harling had watched them for quite some time only an hour ago. Every fourteen minutes the heavy barrel of one of the guns would jerk back under the vicious recoil of the exploding charge. The other three guns would follow suit, each one firing exactly twelve seconds after the preceding shot had been fired. Then there would be quiet again for fourteen minutes. The elevation of the thick barrels showed that the howitzers were shooting at extreme range.

Walter Harling would not have noticed it without being told that all this looked like real war only to civilian eyes; indeed he did not believe it at first when he was told. But then he began to see it, too. The howitzers fired without flash destroyer . . . and the soldiers did not behave as they would have done if countershelling had been expected. The soldiers were sweating, working hard, pounding away at a distant target with the greatest fire rapidity of which their guns were capable. But they did not have to listen for the sound of approaching enemy shells. They never got a "strafing" without due warning.

There was incessant rumble of artillery fire through the famous forest that was now dripping with rain. Many other batteries of heavy howitzers were shooting too, all firing beautifully synchronized so that there was never a longer interval than fifteen seconds without at least one shell in the air. It sounded almost like the thundering noise of some gigantic machinery, running noisily but steadily.

Suddenly shouts came through the rain, cutting through the artillery noise that almost seemed part of the rainy forest in its monotony.

"Antiaircraft units, attention! Enemy ship approaching!"

The crew of the antiaircraft at once wakened to more intensive life. They grouped around their guns, ready for immediate action, tense with expectation of orders and, possibly, of death.

There were no orders for many minutes. But through the sudden silence that seemingly followed the commotion — the howitzers kept shooting clockwork fashion — Harling heard the deep thunder of much heavier guns. He knew there were several twenty-four-inch railroad guns stationed on the only railroad track that passed near the edge of the national forest.

The heavy, long-range pieces were joining the fire of the howitzers.

The battery commander of the antiaircraft guns, sitting with the earphones of a special detector on his head amidst piles of cartridges, suddenly yelled a series of numbers. Harling understood the meaning of none of them.

"Utmost fire rapidity. Fire!"

The next few minutes were filled by a holocaust

of sound. Four antiaircraft guns began pumping
their shells into the air, forty rounds per minute
each. Other batteries did the same. . . . The forest seemed to be full of hidden antiaircraft units.
Harling looked upward against the rain but it was
impossible to see anything except occasional
flashes of exploding shells. If the enemy ship
passed overhead — as the colonel's detector in
dicated — it was not visible in the rain clouds.

Suddenly the scene was illuminated by a bright
flash, as if at least ten tons of magnesium powder
had exploded. Immediately afterward a ruddy
glow began to show to the left. Trees were burning. But the glow soon died down. The rain was
more effective than the chemical extinguishers
that were probably used by the soldiers close to
the spot where the bolt had struck. The "enemy"
had answered the fire.

An orderly approached Harling.

He saluted, rain dripping from every seam of
his uniform.

"The tanks will be on the road in half an hour,
sir," he reported. "No car can get through," he
added when Harling looked surprised. "After they
have finished unloading ammunition you will
kindly go back with them. The general is expecting you."

"I'll come," said Harling. He said it rather ab-
sent-mindedly because his brain was busy with
very important thoughts. And soon after the order-

ly had left he began walking over the rain-soaked ground of the forest toward the rutted dirt road.

The strange war had started only a few months ago, when Earth had been peaceful and humanity too proud of its achievements for a while to think of destruction. And humanity had even believed itself at the very beginning of a new period, more important than the discovery of the Americas a few centuries back.

But it had really started still further back, although not much more than about a decade. There had been a mighty river winding its way through a long chain of valleys, surrounded by gently sloping mountains. Cedars and pines and a dozen other varieties of trees grew there in abundance. It was a large beautiful forest, so beautiful in fact that the government had deemed it wise to make a national forest out of its most impressive part.

Visitors from all over the country and from quite a number of foreign countries had come to see it. And geologists in summer vacation had worked out its geology, the formations of the valleys and of the river being so interesting to them that the work was really a pleasant hobby. One of the largest valleys had once been an immense lake. Thousands of years ago the river that fed the lake had managed to gnaw a way through a weak spot somewhere in the surrounding mountains, and the lake had emptied first into the next valley and finally across a stretch of desert land into the ocean.

At the spot where the original lake had broken through there was still a large waterfall, not very high but carrying a tremendous volume of water. Engineers had looked at this waterfall occasionally, trying to see whether it might be utilized as a source of electric energy. They had always decided to leave it undisturbed. The difference in level was not very impressive, and there was as yet not much need for electric power in that part of the country.

Then large quantities of bauxite were found only two dozen miles from the waterfall. Thus there arose a need for electric power and finally the government had decided to harness the water power of the river. The reports of the geologists had enabled the technicians to figure out what should be done. The ancient pass, once destroyed by the flow of water from the original lake should be restored, the lake re-created. Then there would be enough electric power for the aluminum industry and still enough water left to irrigate the rather dry areas near the bauxite mines by means of a canal that could at the same time be used to ship ore and aluminum to more densely populated areas of the country.

It was not even very difficult to do all this with the new methods of building developed in similar tasks. While investigations were made, the project

grew. And when the dam was finally built it was
the last word in dam engineering, revolutionary in
construction. As the water in the valley rose, sections could be added to the dam, held in place
by the pressure of the water they confined. Walter Harling, in whose energy and inventive talent
the government had trusted when he had com-
peted with many others for the construction of the
dam was the soul and the brain of the work. And
together with the dam rose his fame. In the end
the Bureau of Reclamation could proudly state
through its public relations office that there was
no bigger artificial lake on Earth, and none that
was as beautiful and as beneficial as this one.
Needless to say that there was also no more modern power plant on Earth, and none that had its
capacity.

Nothing ever went wrong with this power plant.
No matter how the demands of the aluminum
works grew, it quietly and efficiently supplied the
millions of kilowatt hours needed. In the office of
the Treasury nothing but unspoiled pleasure pre-
vailed whenever Harling Dam was mentioned. It
was one of the rare things that were perfect even
in the eyes of the accounting department. The
worst that happened in three and a half years of
successful operation was that somebody managed
to steal ninety thousand kilowatt hours before he
was caught.

Trouble came suddenly and completely one night in spring when the engineers who were sitting quietly and contentedly watching rows of gauges had the feeling of satisfaction that results from an ideal job in ideal surroundings. They felt — and would have said so if they had been asked — that they were living on a perfect planet just at the right time.

Suddenly the needles of the gauges behaved insanely. Those that should have remained at zero showed unbelievable overloads. Others dropped to zero and behaved as if they were desperately trying to indicate negative values. Dozens of warning lights blinked crazily. Almost every warning bell began to ring . . . but not even the noise they made was quite normal; they were ringing sputteringly, in an odd staccato rhythm electric bells are normally not able to produce. The radio that had given forth soft music began to emit sounds that might be a bad imitation of the noise of an artillery barrage.

Telephones were ringing — the same staccato peals, as those of the warning bells — and when the men took the receivers and listened they heard the same thundering noise that came out of the radio's loud-speaker.

As suddenly as it had come it all stopped. The needles of the gauges returned to their normal positions — still quivering a little as if with excitement; the warning bells and the telephones were silent, the warning lights disappeared, and the radio resumed the first movement of the *Moonlight Sonata*. The engineers looked at each other. Nobody said a word because everybody wanted to offer a theory in explanation and nobody could think of one.

Before they had even found time to utter preliminary remarks, the disturbance repeated itself in every detail. But this time the men saw something that they believed to be the cause of these strange happenings. Three dirigibles were cruising at low speed over the forests, headed for the dam and the powerhouse. Then the men saw that they were not dirigibles, but not airplanes either. It was easy to see in the bright light of the full moon that they were entirely different. They looked somewhat like the fuselage of a large airplane.

Their general shape was that of elongated teardrops with circular cross section throughout, tapering to a needle-sharp point. Although the men could see the metal plates that formed the hulls of the ships — they were somewhat scarred and damaged — and although they could count the rows of elliptical portholes, they saw nothing that might support or propel the three ships of the sky. There were no motors, no propellers, not even wings or tail surfaces. Just unsupported beautiful looking hulls, as large as small ocean liners. Occasionally something that looked like luminous spirals appeared near the tail, but it came and went so quickly that the men could not be certain about their observations.

The three ships settled to the ground only about a thousand feet from the powerhouse, coming down as slowly and as gently as airships although they certainly had no gas bags to make them buoyant in air. Most of the men were at the windows now, watching them. They could not see any national insignia, but they assumed these ships to belong to the army of their own nation since there was no reason for an invasion by an enemy. Besides, such invasion would certainly have looked different. Those of the men who had stayed at the gauge panels saw to their utmost surprise that the power output of their power plant began to drop steadily. In less than thirty seconds it had reached zero. A few fuses blew out, for no apparent reason. But the gauges also showed that the turbines and dynamos were still running full speed! It was as if somebody stole all this power before it reached the transmission cables.

Phillips, the chief engineer of the powerhouse, who happened to be on night shift decided to have a closer look at the three ships. He and a number of the others went to the flat roof. The ships were still on the ground when the men arrived on the roof but it seemed that they had drawn closer in the meantime. They were now hardly more than 500 feet from the powerhouse. And then another incredible thing happened, the three ships began to disappear into the ground. It was not very soft ground — it could even bear the weight of a car — but it was by no means rock. And the three ships began to sink down in it as if they were solid and made of lead. When the upper part of their hulls was about even with the surrounding surface they stopped sinking.

Then one of the men made a mistake. There were clouds coming up, obscuring the bright disk of the moon. It became hard to see the incredible ships that had many portholes, not one of them illuminated.

"The searchlights," the man said.

Phillips, the chief engineer, trained the searchlight upon the ships himself. Then somebody closed a switch, and the beam of the searchlight illuminated one of the ships brightly. Something like a bright flash answered. It struck first one of the steel masts supporting the heavy high-tension cables. The mast broke into splinters like a scratched Prince Ruperts Drop. Then the beam struck the powerhouse. And a tenth of a second later every bug and moth sitting on the stones of the walls, every bird and lizard living in the vines that clung to the walls and, of course, every human being inside the house and on the roof were dead.

The next day airplanes came to investigate. The failing of the power had made itself noticeable for hundreds of miles. The fact that no telephone call came from the power plant and that no call could get through was noticed much farther. Therefore airplanes had been dispatched as the swiftest means of investigation. People imagined Harling Dam broken and every soul in the valley drowned. But the pilots of the airplanes that circled over the valleys saw the dam intact and in place. However, they saw a few other things that were unusual. One of the masts was missing, the power cables it had supported were cut and led to three strange things like metal dirigibles, each three-quarters buried in the ground.

These planes did not come back and when they failed to answer radio calls other planes were dispatched. One of them returned, reporting that the other had suddenly broken to pieces in midair when bright flashes from the ground caught them both.

This report stopped further private flying to Harling Dam. The Army took charge of the situation. And three days later quite a bit of information had been gathered . . . while a number of batteries of heavy artillery had arrived in the forest without anybody knowing it.

There were heated discussions at the high-command office.

The facts were clear. But they could not be explained.

Three airships of unknown construction had occupied the nation's largest power plant. They left it running, using the current generated for their own unknown purposes. Airplanes that tried to attack them were doomed — the invaders had an unknown but deadly accurate weapon. But it did not affect all types of planes alike; some had escaped. They were not undamaged but had managed to glide away from the danger zone.

It was found that their motors and some other implements had disappeared, save for a few handfuls of bits of metal found in the casing. Somebody discovered accidentally that these bits were highly magnetized. Somebody else realized that the planes that escaped were those built of metals other than steel. The conclusion was obvious, that the white beam from the three ships destroyed iron and steel. Possibly by setting up such magnetic strains and stresses that the material broke to pieces — although the theory of ferromagnetism could not explain such a procedure — possibly by entirely unknown means that brought magnetization only as a by-product.

The ground investigation units dispatched by the Army reported other strange facts. There seemed to be a zone where life could not exist. This zone was roughly circular — as far as could be found — with the ships as the center of the circle. The zone extended just beyond Harling Dam. Whoever crossed the invisible border line of the zone just dropped dead, nobody could tell why. The soldiers had marked the danger line as well as they could.

Another crew had tried to establish communication by heliograph with the three ships, because they did not answer radio calls. They had answered the call with a bright flash that wiped out crew, heliograph, and car alike. Obviously, bright light was disliked by the occupants of the three ships, or else they confused it with their own destructive beam.

Occasionally one of the three ships rose from its pit and cruised to some other part of the world. They were seen — and if not seen, detected by the very typical "staccato static" radios emitted when one of the ships was near — almost everywhere. One day Hong Kong reported them, the next day London and Berlin, almost simultaneously, then Buenos Aires and New York, with only two and a half hours difference. Nothing ever happened. When airplanes went up to approach them they withdrew to high altitudes where the planes could not follow. Occasionally they flashed what was taken as a mysterious signal, a bright ball of light, that was at first deep violet, changed slowly to blue, and more rapidly through all the other colors of the rainbow, to red.

It was the astronomer Professor Hasgrave who was the first to say publicly what many had been suspecting for many days, that these three ships were arrivals from another planet, possibly even another solar system.

The military authorities who were in charge of the case laughed about Hasgrave at first. But they had to admit that none of their scientists could really explain the feats accomplished by the strangers, to say nothing of duplicating them. They also had to admit that their secret service had not been able to find even the slightest clue that ships of this type had been built in any other country. They began to admit the possibility of extraterrestrial origin of the strange ships when Hasgrave suddenly found a convincing explanation for the bright ball of light released over several cities.

It was not a weapon, he explained, but a warning. It was the adaptation of an astronomical principle for communication. The ball displayed the Doppler effect; it shifted from blue through all colors to red. In astronomy this indicated the recession of a body. Since the sphere of light had remained motionless, it obviously meant that

the airplanes should go. The speed with which
the colors changed increased during the display,
meaning that they should go with increasing
speed.

A few days of mental effort made the authorities realize that the three ships were actually
visitors from the void. To be exact, they were
not really visitors. They had just come and established themselves. They were uncommunica-
tive, in fact, warning humans to stay away. They
did no harm, if not approached. And they did
not take anything away except the current produced in the power plants of Harling Dam. They
behaved actually as a human being might behave at a bee hive. Doing no intentional harm,
just taking honey away and crushing those bees
that disturbed them. But the bees had stings to
defend themselves and to avenge the loss of those
killed. Humanity had stings too, airplanes and
tanks and guns.

Soon men craved for war with the aliens. They
had not come as friends, therefore they must be
enemies. That they were simply indifferent hurt
mankind's pride. They should at least make an
attempt to apologize for the loss of life they had
caused. Intelligent beings who were able to do
what they did would certainly also be able to
communicate if they wanted to. At any event,
they had opened hostilities and had to be shown
that humanity was not afraid to fight.

The general in command of the Armed Forces finally felt convinced that he should order an artillery attack. There were many heavy batteries massed now in the forest.

The general gave the order.

Six eight-inch shells dropped in a steep trajectory on the three ships.

The battery commanders had had weeks of time to work out all the factors determining the trajectories. Five of the six shells made clean hits . . . but they exploded fifty meters above the targets. The sixth shell strayed a bit from its trajectory, it landed a few meters from the powerhouse, digging a large crater and damaging the building slightly.

Twenty-four hours later the general received a report that a dome of silvery metal had been erected overnight. It covered the powerhouse and a trial shot with a single heavy shell proved that this dome was as impervious to shellfire as the ships themselves. Then the strange war had begun in earnest. But it was one-sided for most of the time and absolutely ineffective. The gunners, although they kept up continuous bombardment, did not succeed in catching a ship off guard. The strange power that made shells explode at a safe distance did not fail for a moment. The men grew desperate, especially since the ships occasionally retaliated, always taking a heavy toll of lives and of equipment.

Finally Professor Hasgrave conceived a plan. It was his firm conviction that all these strange manifestations of power were basically electric phenomena. There should be a way of dealing with them. The first man Hasgrave informed was Walter Harling, the man who had created Harling Dam that had become the center of all these strange happenings. They then talked to the general, finally to the president. In the end they agreed to try Hasgrave's plan. And Walter Harling at last won the bitter argument that arose ... he carried it out himself.

The tank, splashing through rain and mud brought Harling to a simple but fairly large building, the home of the rangers of the forest, now serving as headquarters for the military command. The general was waiting for them.

They were standing in the doorway, looking out on the dark and rainy landscape. None of them spoke, each knew what the other was thinking.

"The equipment is ready," said the general finally.

"So am I," answered Harling.

They shook hands.

"Red rockets," said Harling.

"Red rockets," repeated the general. "Good luck, Harling!"

Officers led Harling along a wet concrete road which ended at the shore of Harling Lake. There was a boat waiting on the water. And a squadron of hydroplanes. Harling heard them take off ten minutes after the motor launch had pulled his rowboat from the shore. When the planes were in the air the rumble of artillery fire gradually died down.

Harling knew what was going on in the forest.

Guns were inspected and made ready to fire at a given signal. Ammunition was piled up close to the guns, ready for immediate use. Automatic gyro-controlled devices aligned the barrels of whole batteries on the targets. The gigantic railroad guns, not able to fire quickly, pointed their barrels in such a way that their superheavy shells would land exactly in the right spot at the right moment. Expertly trained officers worked with slide rules to find the right amount of powder needed for a given trajectory at a certain air pressure, density, and temperature.

"Half a mile from the danger zone," said the officer in the motor launch.

"Cut cables!"

"Good luck!"

Harling waited till the motor vessel had disappeared in the rain. Then he inspected his boat. It was built without the tiniest bit of iron. From the sides of the wooden vessel aluminum struts projected upwards, supporting a net of gleaming copper wire. It covered the boat entirely, just high enough for Harling to stand upright in it.

On all sides the copper net trailed in the water, leaving enough room to handle the oars.

Something like a wide cape of copper-wire mesh was ready for Harling. It was supported over his head by struts fastened to a wide aluminum collar. The "cape" was long enough to touch the ground all around his feet in any position Harling might assume. Like the net protecting the boat, it should be heavy enough to ground even powerful electric bolts. Harling donned the strange garment and rowed toward the valve controls of his dam. Meanwhile the airplanes — all aluminum construction, even the motors that naturally did not last very long — danced like fireflies over the three ships and the metal dome that covered the powerhouse. The planes tried to center the enemy's attention upon themselves. If he was attentive to their puny actions at all . . .

When Harling passed the invisible barrier he felt a prickling sensation on his skin. It actually was an electric field of great power, generated and kept up in a manner unknown to terrestrial science. Suddenly the dam appeared out of the darkness, looking like a massive seven-foot wall from the lake. Harling followed its curve with his boat. He knew every inch of this dam — but he had no time for sentimental recollections. He prayed that the valve controls were in working order. They were hydraulic and would not be impaired by the electric field. But the "enemy" might have destroyed them; nobody had ever been able to approach and investigate.

Harling found one of the metal stairways that led from the crown of the dam to the bottom of the lake. He tied the boat to it, made certain that the several dozens of red starlight rockets set up in the copper net were still in proper position. He took the main fuse — electric ignition was, of course, impossible — which was inserted into a watertight rubber hose. There were matches in a watertight case tied to the end of the hose. Harling took the end of the main fuse with him. Then he lifted the net of the boat and stepped on the metal staircase, always careful to have his wire-mesh armor trailing in the water. He waited for electrical effects; there were none.

Fortunately, there was a catwalk running along the inner side of the dam, now submerged under about four feet of water. Harling decided that the submerged catwalk was a still better way than the crown of the dam. He might be seen up there, even if he crawled and in spite of the darkness. Hasgrave had a theory that "those others" might be able to "see" the heat his body radiated.

He held match case and rubber hose in his left hand, heavy service pistol in the other; nobody could know what he might encounter in the valve

house. The door was not closed when he arrived
there at last. The body of a dead man blocked
his way, the guard who had been on duty when
the invaders came. There was no living being in
the four rooms. He looked over the controls; nobody had touched them for weeks and they
seemed to be in working order. He tried one of
the smallest valves experimentally . . . it did
work. He could go through with the original
plan.

He opened the match case. The matches were
dry.

Then he turned the wheels that opened the
upper gates of both spillways. But he did not
open the lower locks that made the water coming through the spillways pour into the canal.
The water would fill both of the gigantic spillways and would stop at the lower lock. If this
lock should give, the water would not enter the
canal that was closed by a second lock, but would
flood the valley itself. Therefore the mechanisms
were set once and for all in such a way that the
lower locks could not be operated independently.
They could only be opened and closed together.
Harling left them all closed as they were according to the instruments on the panel.

He waited for three minutes, knowing that
everything depended on these three times sixty
seconds. A hundred times he thought during the
next hundred and fifty seconds that his watch

had stopped. A hundred times he made sure that it had not.

Everywhere in the forest the officers of the gun crews were waiting too, eyes glued to the dials of the watches, hands ready to pull the lanyards of their pieces. Crack pilots, while doing crazy stunts with their hydroplanes above the quietly resting three alien ships, glanced at the crown of the dam.

Two minutes and forty seconds.

Countless tons of water were falling down the steep grading of the tubular spillways.

Two minutes and forty-five seconds.

More and more water going into the spillways. The level of the lake actually receding by inches, unobservable due to the beating rain.

Two minutes and fifty seconds.

The water must reach the lower locks in twenty seconds. Three seconds . . . one had to allow for the fuse to burn, one or two for the rockets, four more for . . .

Two minutes and fifty-five seconds.

Harling lighted six or seven matches in a bundle, held the rubber hose clenched.

Three minutes!

Now two more seconds to wait. Harling counted them with a strained voice counting not "one, two," but higher figures that would take a second to pronounce.

"A hundred and one" . . . "A hundred and two" . . .

He lighted the fuse, let it fall to the floor and threw himself down.

Three seconds later five dozen Army rockets rose into the sky. Though wet, most of them worked. They fought their way through the rain . . . Harling thought that the resistance of the rain was very fortunate, else they might explode in the deep hanging clouds and go unnoticed.

The sky suddenly shone red with Very lights.

Like a mighty thunderclap four-score guns answered, barrels jerking back under the recoil, reports deafening crews, shells screaming through the rain.

The shells of the howitzers arrived first, exploding over their usual targets, ships and dome. A second later the twenty-four-inch projectiles of the railroad guns came. They were aimed with deadly accuracy. Two on each side of the valley arrived side by side . . .

And broke the lower locks!

A flood of water spouted out of the spillways, spread over the valley because the second locks, those closing the canal, still blocked the way. At the same instant the shells of two combined batteries of seventeen-inch mobile mortars crashed into the dam — where sections joined that were not so stable now under lessening water pressure. Harling Dam broke, thundered down into the valley.

It poured over the dome and the ships. And together with the water came all the shells the already steaming barrels of dozens of batteries of heavy howitzers had held in reserve.

And Professor Hasgrave proved to be right again. The repellent shield on which shells and bombs had exploded was gone, somehow the water made its power fail. The avalanche of heavy shells exploded on the hulls and inside of their targets. The targets ceased to exist . . . .

The general himself was present in the rescue party that climbed up to the valve tower in search of Harling. They did not have a very clear conception what they had expected to see . . . at any event it was not what they really saw.

Harling was sitting with only very little clothing — the other hung over the rail to dry — in the rays of the early morning sun at the only table in the control room. He was furiously writing equations on the back of beer advertising posters. And instead of listening to congratulations, he informed the rescue party that Harling Dam could be ready to resume work before spring.

It's Such
A Beautiful Day

by Isaac Asimov

ON APRIL 12, 2117, the field-modulator brake-valve in the Door belonging to Mrs. Richard Hanshaw depolarized for reasons unknown. As a result, Mrs. Hanshaw's day was completely upset and her son, Richard, Jr., first developed his strange neurosis.

It was not the type of thing you would find listed as a neurosis in the usual textbooks and certainly young Richard behaved, in most respects, just as a well-brought-up twelve-year-old in prosperous circumstances ought to behave.

And yet from April 12 on, Richard Hanshaw, Jr., could only with regret ever persuade himself to go through a Door.

Of all this, on April 12, Mrs. Hanshaw had no

premonition. She woke in the morning (an ordinary morning) as her mekkano slithered gently into her room, with a cup of coffee on a small tray. Mrs. Hanshaw was planning a visit to New York in the afternoon and she had several things to do first that could not quite be trusted to a mekkano, so after one or two sips, she stepped out of bed.

The mekkano backed away, moving silently along the diamagnetic field that kept its oblong body half an inch above the floor, and moved back to the kitchen, where its simple computer was quite adequate to set the proper controls on the various kitchen appliances in order that an appropriate breakfast might be prepared.

Mrs. Hanshaw, having bestowed the usual sentimental glance upon the cubograph of her dead husband, passed through the stages of her morning ritual with a certain contentment. She could hear her son across the hall clattering through his, but she knew she need not interfere with him. The mekkano was well adjusted to see to it, as a matter of course, that he was showered, that he had on a change of clothing, and that he would eat a nourishing breakfast. The tergo-shower she had had installed the year before made the morning wash and dry so quick and pleasant that, really, she felt certain Dickie would wash even without supervision.

On a morning like this, when she was busy, it

would certainly not be necessary for her to do more than deposit a casual peck on the boy's cheek before he left. She heard the soft chime the mekkano sounded to indicate approaching school time and she floated down the force lift to the lower floor (her hair style for the day only sketchily designed, as yet) in order to perform that motherly duty.

She found Richard standing at the Door, with his textreels and pocket projector dangling by their strap and a frown on his face.

"Say, Mom," he said, looking up, "I dialed the school's co-ords but nothing happens."

She said, almost automatically, "Nonsense, Dickie. I never heard of such a thing."

"Well, you try."

Mrs. Hanshaw tried a number of times. Strange, the school Door was always set for general reception. She tried other co-ordinates. Her friends' Doors might not be set for reception, but there would be a signal at least, and then she could explain.

But nothing happened at all. The Door remained an inactive gray barrier despite all her manipulations. It was obvious that the Door was out of order—and only five months after its annual fall inspection by the company.

She was quite angry about it.

It *would* happen on a day when she had much planned. She thought petulantly of the fact that a month earlier she had decided against installing a subsidiary Door on the ground that it was an unnecessary expense. How was she to know that Doors were getting to be so *shoddy*?

She stepped to the visiphone while the anger still burned in her and said to Richard, "You just go down the road, Dickie, and use the Williamsons' Door."

Ironically, in view of later developments, Richard balked. "Aw, gee, Mom, I'll get dirty. Can't I stay home till the Door is fixed?"

And, as ironically, Mrs. Hanshaw insisted. With her finger on the combination board of the phone, she said, "You won't get dirty if you put flexies on your shoes, and don't forget to brush yourself well before you go into their house."

"But, golly—"

"No back talk, Dickie. You've got to be in school. Just let me see you walk out of here. And quickly, or you'll be late."

The mekkano, an advanced model and very responsive, was already standing before Richard with flexies in one appendage.

Richard pulled the transparent plastic shields over his shoes and moved down the hall with visible reluctance. "I don't even know how to work this thing, Mom."

"You just push that button," Mrs. Hanshaw called. "The red button. Where it says 'For Emergency Use.' And don't dawdle. Do you want the mekkano to go along with you?"

"Gosh, no," he called back, morosely, "what do you think I am? A baby? Gosh!" His muttering was cut off by a slam.

With flying fingers, Mrs. Hanshaw punched the appropriate combination on the phone board and thought of the things she intended saying to the company about this.

Joe Bloom, a reasonably young man, who had gone through technology school with added training in force-field mechanics, was at the Hanshaw residence in less than half an hour. He was really quite competent, though Mrs. Hanshaw regarded his youth with deep suspicion.

She opened the movable house panel when he first signaled and her sight of him was as he stood there, brushing at himself vigorously to remove the dust of the open air. He took off his flexies and dropped them where he stood. Mrs. Hanshaw closed the house panel against the flash of raw sunlight that had entered. She found herself irrationally hoping that the step-by-step trip from the public Door had been an unpleasant one. Or perhaps that the public Door itself had been out of order and the youth had had to lug his tools even farther than the necessary two hundred yards. She wanted the Company, or its representative at least, to suffer a bit. It would teach them what broken Doors meant.

But he seemed cheerful and unperturbed as he said, "Good morning, ma'am. I came to see about your Door."

"I'm glad someone did," said Mrs. Hanshaw, ungraciously. "My day is quite ruined."

"Sorry, ma'am. What seems to be the trouble?"

"It just won't work. Nothing at all happens when you adjust co-ords," said Mrs. Hanshaw. "There was no warning at all. I had to send my son out to the neighbors through that — that thing."

She pointed to the entrance through which the repair man had come.

He smiled and spoke out of the conscious wisdom of his own specialized training in Doors. "That's a door, too, ma'am. You don't give that kind a capital letter when you write it. It's a hand-door, sort of. It used to be the only kind once."

"Well, at least it works. My boy's had to go out in the dirt and germs."

"It's not bad outside today, ma'am," he said, with the connoisseur-like air of one whose profession forced him into the open nearly every day. "Sometimes it *is* real unpleasant. But I guess you want I should fix this here Door, ma'am, so I'll get on with it."

He sat down on the floor, opened the large tool case he had brought in with him and in half a minute, by use of a point demagnetizer, he had the control panel removed and a set of intricate vitals exposed.

He whistled to himself as he placed the fine electrodes of the field analyzer on numerous points, studying the shifting needles on the dials. Mrs. Hanshaw watched him, arms folded.

Finally, he said, "Well, here's something," and with a deft twist, he disengaged the brake valve.

He tapped it with a fingernail and said, "This here brake valve is depolarized, ma'am. There's your whole trouble." He ran his finger along the little pigeonholes in his tool case and lifted out a duplicate of the object he had taken from the door mechanism. "These things just go all of a sudden. Can't predict it."

He put the control panel back and stood up. "It'll work now, ma'am."

He punched a reference combination, blanked it, then punched another. Each time, the dull gray of the Door gave way to a deep, velvety blackness. He said, "Will you sign here, ma'am? and put down your charge number, too, please? Thank you, ma'am."

He punched a new combination, that of his home factory, and with a polite touch of finger to forehead, he stepped through the Door. As his body entered the blackness, it was cut off sharply. Less and less of him was visible and the tip of his tool case was the last thing that showed. A second after he had passed through completely, the Door turned back to dull gray.

Half an hour later, when Mrs. Hanshaw had

finally completed her interrupted preparations and was fuming over the misfortune of the morning, the phone buzzed annoyingly and her real troubles began.

Miss Elizabeth Robbins was distressed. Little Dick Hanshaw had always been a good pupil. She hated to report him like this. And yet, she told herself, his actions were certainly queer. And she would talk to his mother, not to the principal.

She slipped out to the phone during the morning study period, leaving a student in charge. She made her connection and found herself staring at Mrs. Hanshaw's handsome and somewhat formidable head.

Miss Robbins quailed, but it was too late to turn back. She said, diffidently, "Mrs. Hanshaw, I'm Miss Robbins." She ended on a rising note.

Mrs. Hanshaw looked blank, then said, "Richard's teacher?" That, too, ended on a rising note.

"That's right. I called you, Mrs. Hanshaw," Miss Robbins plunged right into it, "to tell you that Dick was quite late to school this morning."

"He *was*?" But that couldn't be. I saw him leave."

Miss Robbins looked astonished. She said, "You mean you saw him use the Door?"

Mrs. Hanshaw said quickly, "Well, no. Our Door was temporarily out of order. I sent him to a neighbor and he used that Door."

"Are you sure?"

"Of course I'm sure. I wouldn't lie to you."

"No, no, Mrs. Hanshaw. I wasn't implying that at all. I meant are you sure he found the way to the neighbor? He might have got lost."

"Ridiculous. We have the proper maps, and I'm sure Richard knows the location of every house in District A-3." Then, with the quiet pride of one who knows what is her due, she added, "Not that he ever needs to know, of course. The co-ords are all that are necessary at any time."

Miss Robbins, who came from a family that had always had to economize rigidly on the use of its Doors (the price of power being what it was) and who had therefore run errands on foot until quite an advanced age, resented the pride. She said, quite clearly, "Well, I'm afraid, Mrs. Hanshaw, that Dick did not use the neighbor's Door. He was over an hour late to school and the condition of his flexies made it quite obvious that he tramped cross-country. They were *muddy*."

"*Muddy?*" Mrs. Hanshaw repeated the emphasis on the word. "What did he say? What was his excuse?"

Miss Robbins couldn't help but feel a little glad at the discomfiture of the other woman. She said, "He wouldn't talk about it. Frankly, Mrs. Hanshaw, he seems ill. That's why I called you. Perhaps you might want to have a doctor look at him."

"Is he running a temperature?" The mother's voice went shrill.

"Oh, no. I don't mean physically ill. It's just his attitude and the look in his eyes." She hesitated, then said with every attempt at delicacy, "I thought perhaps a routine checkup with a psychic probe —"

She didn't finish. Mrs. Hanshaw, in a chilled voice and with what was as close to a snort as her breeding would permit, said, "Are you implying that Richard is *neurotic*?"

"Oh, no, Mrs. Hanshaw, but —"

"It certainly sounded so. The idea! He has always been perfectly healthy. I'll take this up with him when he gets home. I'm sure there's a perfectly normal explanation which he'll give to *me*."

The connection broke abruptly, and Miss Robbins felt hurt and uncommonly foolish. After all, she had only tried to help, to fulfill what she considered an obligation to her students.

She hurried back to the classroom with a glance at the metal face of the wall clock. The study period was drawing to an end. English composition next.

But her mind wasn't completely on English composition. Automatically, she called the students to have them read selections from their literary creations. And occasionally she punched one of those selections on tape and ran it through the small vocalizer to show the students how English *should* be read.

The vocalizer's mechanical voice, as always, dripped perfection, but, again as always, lacked character. Sometimes, she wondered if it was wise to try to train the students into a speech that was divorced from individuality and geared only to a mass-average accent and intonation.

Today, however, she had no thought for that. It was Richard Hanshaw she watched. He sat quietly in his seat, quite obviously indifferent to his surroundings. He was lost deep in himself and just not the same boy he had been. It was obvious to her that he had had some unusual experience that morning and, really, she was right to call his mother, although perhaps she ought not to have made the remark about the probe. Still it was quite the thing these days. All sorts of people got probed. There wasn't any disgrace attached to it. Or there shouldn't be, anyway.

She called on Richard, finally. She had to call twice, before he responded and rose to his feet.

The general subject assigned had been: "If you had your choice of traveling on some ancient vehicle, which would you choose, and why?" Miss Robbins tried to use the topic every semester. It was a good one because it carried a sense of history with it. It forced the youngsters to think about the manner of living of people in past ages.

She listened while Richard Hanshaw read in a low voice.

"If I had my choice of ancient vehicles," he said, pronouncing the "h" in vehicles. "I would choose the stratoliner. It travels slow like all vehicles but it is clean. Because it travels in the stratosphere, it must be all enclosed so that you are not likely to catch disease. You can see the stars if it is nighttime almost as good as in a planetarium. If you look down you can see the Earth like a map or maybe see clouds — " He went on for several hundred more words.

She said brightly when he had finished reading, "It's pronounced *vee*-ick-ulls, Richard. No 'h.' Accent on the first syllable. And you don't say 'travels slow' or 'see good.' What do you say, class?"

There was a small chorus of responses and she went on. "That's right. Now what is the difference between an adjective and an adverb? Who can tell me?"

And so it went. Lunch passed. Some pupils stayed to eat; some went home. Richard stayed. Miss Robbins noted that; usually he didn't.

The afternoon passed, too, and then there was the final bell and the usual upsurging hum as twenty-five boys and girls rattled their belongings together and took their leisurely place in line.

Miss Robbins clapped her hands together. "Quickly, children. Come, Zelda, take your place."

"I dropped my tape-punch, Miss Robbins," shrilled the girl, defensively.

"Well, pick it up, pick it up. Now children, be brisk, be brisk."

She pushed the button that slid a section of the wall into a recess and revealed the gray blankness of a large Door. It was not the usual Door that the occasional student used in going home for lunch, but an advanced model that was one of the prides of this well-to-do private school.

In addition to its double width, it possessed a large and impressively gear-filled "automatic serial finder" which was capable of adjusting the door for a number of different co-ordinates at automatic intervals.

At the beginning of the semester, Miss Robbins always had to spend an afternoon with the mechanic, adjusting the device for the co-ordinates of the homes of the new class. But then, thank goodness, it rarely needed attention for the remainder of the term.

The class lined up alphabetically, first girls, then boys. The door went velvety black and Hester Adams waved her hand and stepped through. " 'By-y-y——"

"The " 'bye" was cut off in the middle, as it almost always was.

The door went gray, then black again, and Theresa Cantrocchi went through. Gray, black, Zelda

Charlowicz. Gray, black, Patricia Coombs. Gray, black, Sara May Evans.

The line grew smaller as the Door swallowed them one by one, depositing each in her home. Of course, an occasional mother forgot to leave the house Door on special reception at the appropriate time and then the school Door remained gray. Automatically, after a minute-long wait, the Door went on to the next combination in line and the pupil in question had to wait till it was all over, after which a phone call to the forgetful parent would set things right. This was always bad for the pupils involved, especially the sensitive ones who took seriously the implication that they were little thought of at home. Miss Robbins always tried to impress this on visiting parents, but it happened at least once every semester just the same.

The girls were all through, now. John Abramowitz stepped through and then Edwin Byrne—

Of course, another trouble, and a more frequent one was the boy or girl who got into line out of place. They *would* do it despite the teacher's sharpest watch, particularly at the beginning of the term when the proper order was less familiar to them.

When that happened, children would be popping into the wrong houses by the half dozen and would have to be sent back. It always meant a mixup that took minutes to straighten out and parents were invariably irate.

Miss Robbins was suddenly aware that the line had stopped. She spoke sharply to the boy at the head of the line.

"Step through, Samuel. What are you waiting for?"

Samuel Jones raised a complacent countenance and said, "It's not my combination, Miss Robins."

"Well, whose is it?" She looked impatiently down the line of five remaining boys. Who was out of place?"

"It's Dick Hanshaw's, Miss Robbins."

"Where is he?"

Another boy answered, with the rather repulsive tone of self-righteousness all children automatically assume in reporting the deviations of their friends to elders in authority, "He went through the fire door, Miss Robbins."

"What?"

The schoolroom Door had passed onto another combination and Samuel Jones passed through. One by one, the rest followed.

Miss Robbins was alone in the classroom. She stepped to the fire door. It was a small affair, manually operated, and hidden behind a bend in the wall so that it would not break up the uniform structure of the room.

She opened it a crack. It was there as a means of escape from the building in case of fire, a device which was enforced by an anachronistic law that did not take into account the modern methods of automatic fire fighting that all public buildings used. There was nothing outside but the outside. The sunlight was harsh and a dusty wind was blowing.

Miss Robbins closed the door. She was glad she had called Mrs. Hanshaw. She had done her duty. More than ever, it was obvious that something was wrong with Richard. She suppressed the impulse to phone again.

Mrs. Hanshaw did not go to New York that day. She remained home in a mixture of anxiety and an irrational anger, the latter directed against the impudent Miss Robbins.

Some fifteen minutes before school's end, her anxiety drove her to the Door. Last year she had had it equipped with an automatic device which activated it to the school's co-ordinates at five of three and kept it so, barring manual adjustment, until Richard arrived.

Her eyes were fixed on the Door's dismal gray (why couldn't an inactive force-field be any other color, something more lively and cheerful?) and waited. Her hands felt cold as she squeezed them together.

The Door turned black at the precise second but nothing happened. The minutes passed and Richard was late. Then quite late. Then very late.

It was a quarter of four and she was distracted. Normally, she would have phoned the school, but she couldn't, she couldn't. Not after that teacher had deliberately cast doubts on Richard's mental well-being. How could she?

Mrs. Hanshaw moved about restlessly, lighting a cigarette with fumbling fingers, then smudging it out. Could it be something quite normal? Could Richard be staying after school for some reason? Surely he would have told her in advance. A gleam of light struck her; he knew she was planning to go to New York and might not be back till late in the evening —

No, he would surely have told her. Why fool herself?

Her pride was breaking. She would have to call the school, or even (she closed her eyes and teardrops squeezed through between the lashes) the police.

And when she opened her eyes, Richard stood before her, eyes on the ground and his whole bearing that of someone waiting for a blow to fall.

"Hello, Mom."

Mrs. Hanshaw's anxiety transmuted itself instantly (in a manner known only to mothers) to anger. "Where have you been, Richard?"

And then, before she could go further into the refrain concerning careless, unthinking sons and broken-hearted mothers, she took note of his appearance in greater detail, and gasped in utter horror.

She said, "You've been in the open."

Her son looked down at his dusty shoes (minus flexies), at the dirt marks that streaked his lower arms and at the small, but definite tear in his shirt. He said, "Gosh, Mom, I just thought I'd — " and he faded out.

She said, "Was there anything wrong with the school Door?"

"No, Mom."

"Do you realize I've been worried sick about you?" She waited vainly for an answer. "Well, I'll talk to you afterward, young man. First, you're taking a bath, and every stitch of your clothing is being thrown out. Mekkano!"

But the mekkano had already reacted properly to the phrase "taking a bath" and was off to the bathroom in its silent glide.

"You take your shoes off right here," said Mrs. Hanshaw, "then march after mekkano."

Richard did as he was told with a resignation that placed him beyond futile protest.

Mrs. Hanshaw picked up the soiled shoes between thumb and forefinger and dropped them down the disposal chute which hummed in faint dismay at the unexpected load. She dusted her hands carefully on a tissue which she allowed to float down the chute after the shoes.

She did not join Richard at dinner but let him

eat in the worse-than-lack-of-company of the mek-kano. This, she thought, would be an active sign of her displeasure and would do more than any amount of scolding or punishment to make him realize that he had done wrong. Richard, she frequently told herself, was a sensitive boy.

But she went up to see him at bedtime.

She smiled at him and spoke softly. She thought that would be the best way. After all, he had been punished already.

She said, "What happened today, Dickie-boy?" She had called him that when he was a baby and just the sound of the name softened her nearly to tears.

But he only looked away and his voice was stubborn and cold. "I just don't like to go through those darn Doors, Mom."

"But why ever not?"

He shuffled his hands over the filmy sheet (fresh, clean, antiseptic and, of course, disposable after each use) and said, "I just don't like them."

"But then how do you expect to go to school, Dickie?"

"I'll get up early," he mumbled.

"But there's nothing wrong with Doors."

"Don't like 'em." He never once looked up at her.

She said, despairingly, "Oh, well, you have a good sleep and tomorrow morning you'll feel much better."

She kissed him and left the room, automatically passing her hand through the photo-cell beam and in that manner dimming the roomlights.

But she had trouble sleeping herself that night. Why should Dickie dislike Doors so suddenly? They had never bothered him before. To be sure, the Door had broken down in the morning but that should make him appreciate them all the more.

Dickie was behaving so unreasonably.

Unreasonably? That reminded her of Miss Robbins and her diagnosis and Mrs. Hanshaw's soft jaw set in the darkness and privacy of her bedroom. Nonsense! The boy was upset and a night's sleep was all the therapy he needed.

But the next morning when she arose, her son was not in the house. The mekkano could not speak but it could answer questions with gestures of its appendages equivalent to a yes or no, and it did not take Mrs. Hanshaw more than half a minute to ascertain that the boy had arisen thirty minutes earlier than usual, skimped his shower, and darted out of the house.

But not by way of the Door.

Out the other way — through the door. Small "d."

Mrs. Hanshaw's visiphone signaled genteelly at 3:10 P.M. that day. Mrs. Hanshaw guessed the caller and having activated the receiver, saw that she had guessed correctly. A quick glance in the mirror to see that she was properly calm after a day of abstracted concern and worry and then she keyed in her own transmission.

"Yes, Miss Robbins," she said coldly.

Richard's teacher was a bit breathless. She said, "Mrs. Hanshaw, Richard has deliberately left through the fire door although I told him to use the regular Door. I do not know where he went."

Mrs. Hanshaw said, carefully, "He left to come home."

Miss Robbins looked dismayed, "Do you approve of this?"

Pale-faced, Mrs. Hanshaw set about putting the teacher in her place. "I don't think it is up to you to criticize. If my son does not choose to use the Door, it is his affair and mine. I don't think there is any school ruling that would force him to use the Door, is there?" Her bearing quite plainly intimated that if there were she would see to it that it was changed.

Miss Robbins flushed and had time for one quick remark before contact was broken. She said, "I'd have him probed. I really would."

Mrs. Hanshaw remained standing before the quartzinium plate, staring blindly at its blank face. Her sense of family placed her for a few moments quite firmly on Richard's side. Why *did* he have to use the Door if he chose not to? And then she settled down to wait and pride battled the gnawing anxiety that something after all was wrong with Richard.

He came home with a look of defiance on his face, but his mother, with a strenuous effort at self-control, met him as though nothing were out of the ordinary.

For weeks, she followed that policy. It's nothing, she told herself. It's a vagary. He'll grow out of it.

It grew into an almost normal state of affairs. Then, too, every once in a while, perhaps three days in a row, she would come down to breakfast to find Richard waiting sullenly at the Door, then using it when school time came. She always refrained from commenting on the matter.

Always, when he did that, and especially when he followed it up by arriving home via the Door, her heart grew warm and she thought, "Well, it's over." But always with the passing of one day, two or three, he would return like an addict to his drug and drift silently out by the door — small "d" — before she woke.

And each time she thought despairingly of psychiatrists and probes, and each time the vision of Miss Robbins' low-bred staisfaction at (possibly) learning of it, stopped her, although she was scarcely aware that that was the true motive.

Meanwhile, she lived with it and made the best of it. The mekkano was instructed to wait at the door — small "d" — with a Tergo kit and a change of clothing. Richard washed and changed without resistance. His underthings, socks, and flexies were disposable in any case, and Mrs. Hanshaw bore uncomplainingly the expense of daily disposal of shirts. Trousers she finally allowed to go a week before disposal on condition of rigorous nightly cleaning.

One day she suggested that Richard accompany her on a trip to New York. It was more a vague desire to keep him in sight than part of any purposeful plan. He did not object. He was even happy. He stepped right through the Door, unconcerned. He didn't hesitate. He even lacked the look of resentment he wore on those mornings he used the Door to go to school.

Mrs. Hanshaw rejoiced. This could be a way of weaning him back into Door usage, and she racked her ingenuity for excuses to make trips with Richard. She even raised her power bill to quite unheard-of heights by suggesting, and going through with, a trip to Canton for the day in order to witness a Chinese festival.

That was on a Sunday, and the next morning Richard marched directly to the hole in the wall he always used. Mrs. Hanshaw, having wakened particularly early, witnessed that. For once, badgered past endurance, she called after him plaintively, "Why not the Door, Dickie?"

He said, briefly, "It's all right for Canton," and stepped out of the house.

So that plan ended in failure. And then, one day, Richard came home soaking wet. The mekkano hovered about him uncertainly and Mrs. Hanshaw, just returned from a four-hour visit with her sister in Iowa, cried, "Richard Hanshaw!"

He said, hang-dog fashion, "It started raining. All of a sudden, it started raining."

For a moment, the word didn't register with her. Her own school days and her studies of geography were twenty years in the past. And then she remembered and caught the vision of water pouring recklessly and endlessly down from the sky — a mad cascade of water with no tap to turn off, no button to push, no contact to break.

She said, "And you stayed out in it?"

He said, "Well, gee, Mom, I came home fast as I could. I didn't know it was going to rain."

Mrs. Hanshaw had nothing to say. She was appalled and the sensation filled her too full for words to find a place.

Two days later, Richard found himself with a running nose, and a dry, scratchy throat. Mrs. Hanshaw had to admit that the virus of disease had found a lodging in her house, as though it were a miserable hovel of the Iron Age.

It was over that that her stubbornness and pride

broke and she admitted to herself that, after all, Richard had to have psychiatric help.

Mrs. Hanshaw chose a psychiatrist with care. Her first impulse was to find one at a distance. For a while, she considered stepping directly into the San Francisco Medical Center and choosing one at random.

And then it occurred to her that by doing that she would merely become an anonymous consultant. She would have no way of obtaining any greater consideration for herself than would be forthcoming to any public-Door user of the city slums. Now if she remained in her own community, her word would carry weight —

She consulted the district map. It was one of that excellent series prepared by Doors, Inc., and distributed free of charge to their clients. Mrs. Hanshaw couldn't quite suppress that little thrill of civic pride as she unfolded the map. It wasn't a fine-print directory of Door co-ordinates only. It was an actual map, with each house carefully located.

And why not? District A-3 was a name of moment in the world, a badge of aristocracy. It was the first community on the planet to have been established on a completely Doored basis. The first, the largest, the wealthiest, the best-known. It needed no factories, no stores. It didn't even need roads. Each house was a little secluded castle, the Door of which had entry anywhere the world over where other Doors existed.

Carefully, she followed down the keyed listing of five thousand families of District A-3. She knew it included several psychiatrists. The learned professions were well represented in A-3.

Doctor Hamilton Sloane was the second name she arrived at and her finger lingered upon the map. His office was scarcely two miles from the Hanshaw residence. She liked his name. The fact that he lived in A-3 was evidence of worth. And he was a neighbor, practically a neighbor. He would understand that it was a matter of urgency, and confidential.

Firmly, she put in a call to his office to make an appointment.

Doctor Hamilton Sloane was a comparatively young man, not quite forty. He was of good family and he had indeed heard of Mrs. Hanshaw.

He listened to her quietly and then said, "And this all began with the Door breakdown."

"That's right, Doctor."

"Does he show any fear of the Doors?"

"Of course not. What an idea!" She was plainly startled.

"It's possible, Mrs. Hanshaw, it's possible. After all, when you stop to think of how a Door works it is rather a frightening thing, really. You step into a Door, and for an instant your atoms are converted into field-energies, transmitted to another part of space and reconverted into matter. For that instant you're not alive."

"I'm sure no one thinks of such things."

"But your son may. He witnessed the breakdown of the Door. He may be saying to himself, 'What if the Door breaks down just as I'm halfway through?'"

"But that's nonsense. He still uses the Door. He's even been to Canton with me; Canton, China. And as I told you, he uses it for school about once or twice a week."

"Freely? Cheerfully?"

"Well," said Mrs. Hanshaw, reluctantly, "he does seem a bit put out by it. But really, Doctor, there isn't much use talking about it, is there? If you would do a quick probe, see where the trouble was," and she finished on a bright note, "why, that would be all. I'm sure it's quite a minor thing."

Dr. Sloane sighed. He detested the word "probe" and there was scarcely any word heard oftener.

"Mrs. Hanshaw," he said patiently, "there is no such thing as a quick probe. Now I know the mag-strips are full of it and it's a rage in some circles, but it's much overrated."

"Are you serious?"

"Quite. The probe is very complicated and the

theory is that it traces mental circuits. You see, the cells of the brains are interconnected in a large variety of ways. Some of those interconnected paths are more used than others. They represent habits of thought, both conscious and unconscious. Theory has it that these paths in any given brain can be used to diagnose mental ills early and with certainty."

"Well, then?"

"But subjection to the probe is quite a fearful thing, especially to a child. It's a traumatic experience. It takes over an hour. And even then, the results must be sent to the Central Psychoanalytical Bureau for analysis, and that could take weeks. And on top of all that, Mrs. Hanshaw, there are many psychiatrists who think the theory of probe analyses to be most uncertain."

Mrs. Hanshaw compressed her lips. "You mean nothing can be done."

Dr. Sloane smiled. "Not at all. There were psychiatrists for centuries before there were probes. I suggest that you let me talk to the boy."

"Talk to him? Is that all?"

"I'll come to you for background information when necessary, but the essential thing, I think, is to talk to the boy."

"Really, Dr. Sloane, I doubt if he'll discuss the matter with you. He won't talk to me about it and I'm his mother."

"That often happens," the psychiatrist assured

her. "A child will sometimes talk more readily to a stranger. In any case, I cannot take the case otherwise."

Mrs. Hanshaw rose, not at all pleased. "When can you come, Doctor?"

"What about this coming Saturday? The boy won't be in school. Will you be busy?"

"We will be ready."

She made a dignified exit. Dr. Sloane accompanied her through the small reception room to his office Door and waited while she punched the co-ordinates of her house. He watched her pass through. She became a half-woman, a quarter-woman, an isolated elbow and foot, a nothing.

It *was* frightening.

Did a Door ever break down during passage, leaving half a body here and half there? He had never heard of such a case, but he imagined it could happen.

He returned to his desk and looked up the time of his next appointment. It was obvious to him that Mrs. Hanshaw was annoyed and disappointed at not having arranged for a psychic probe treatment.

Why? Why should a thing like a probe, an obvious piece of quackery in his own opinion, get such a hold on the general public? It must be part of this general trend toward machines. Anything man can do, machines can do better. Machines! More machines! Machines for anything and everything! O tempora! O mores!

His resentment of the probe was beginning to bother him. Was it a fear of technological unemployment, a basic insecurity on his part, a mechanophobia, if that was the word —

He made a mental note to discuss this with his own analyst.

Dr. Sloane had to feel his way. The boy wasn't a patient who had come to him, more or less anxious to talk, more or less eager to be helped.

Under the circumstances it would have been best to keep his first meeting with Richard short and noncommittal. It would have been sufficient merely to establish himself as something less than a total stranger. The next time he would be someone Richard had seen before. The time after he would be an acquaintance, and after that a friend of the family.

Unfortunately, Mrs. Hanshaw was not likely to accept a long-drawn-out process. She would go searching for a probe and, of course, she would find it.

And harm the boy. He was certain of that.

It was for that reason he felt he must sacrifice a little of the proper caution and risk a small crisis.

An uncomfortable ten minutes had passed when he decided he must try. Mrs. Hanshaw was smiling in a rather rigid way, eyeing him narrowly, as though she expected verbal magic from him. Richard wriggled in his seat, unresponsive to Dr. Sloane's tentative comments, overcome with boredom and unable not to show it.

Dr. Sloane said, with casual suddenness, "Would you like to take a walk with me, Richard?"

The boy's eyes widened and he stopped wriggling. He looked directly at Dr. Sloane. "A walk, sir?"

"I mean, outside."

"Do you go — outside?"

"Sometimes. When I feel like it."

Richard was on his feet, holding down a squirming eagerness. "I didn't think anyone did."

"I do. And I like company."

The boy sat down, uncertainly. "Mom? — "

Mrs. Hanshaw had stiffened in her seat, her compressed lips radiating horror, but she managed to say, "Why certainly, Dickie. But watch yourself."

And she managed a quick and baleful glare at Dr. Sloane.

In one respect, Dr. Sloane had lied. He did *not* go outside "sometimes." He hadn't been in the open since early college days. True, he had been athletically inclined (still was to some extent) but in his time the indoor ultraviolet chambers, swimming pools, and tennis courts had flourished. For those with the price, they were much more satisfactory than the outdoor equivalents, open to the elements as they were, could possibly be. There was no occasion to go outside.

So there was a crawling sensation about his skin when he felt wind touch it, and he put down his flexied shoes on bare grass with a gingerly movement.

"Hey, look at that." Richard was quite different now, laughing, his reserve broken down.

Dr. Sloane had time only to catch a flash of blue that ended in a tree. Leaves rustled and he lost it.

"What was it?"

"A bird," said Richard. "A blue kind of bird."

Dr. Sloane looked about him in amazement. The Hanshaw residence was on a rise of ground, and he could see for miles. The area was only lightly wooded and between clumps of trees, grass gleamed brightly in the sunlight.

Colors set in deeper green made red and yellow patterns. They were flowers. From the books he had viewed in the course of his lifetime and from the old video shows, he had learned enough so that all this had an eerie sort of familiarity.

And yet the grass was so trim, the flowers so patterned. Dimly, he realized he had been expecting something wilder. He said, "Who takes care of all this?"

Richard shrugged. "I dunno. Maybe the mekkanos do it."

"Mekkanos?"

"There's loads of them around. Sometimes they got a sort of atomic knife they hold near the ground. It cuts the grass. And they're always fooling around with the flowers and things. There's one of them over there."

It was a small object, half a mile away. Its metal skin cast back highlights as it moved slowly over the gleaming meadow, engaged in some sort of activity that Dr. Sloane could not identify.

Dr. Sloane was astonished. Here it was a perverse sort of estheticism, a kind of conspicuous consumption —

"What's that?" he asked suddenly.

Richard looked. He said, "That's a house. Belongs to the Froehlichs. Co-ordinates, A-3, 23, 461. That little pointy building over there is the public Door."

Dr. Sloane was staring at the house. Was that what it looked like from the outside? Somehow he had imagined something more cubic, and taller.

"Come along," shouted Richard, running ahead.

Dr. Sloane followed more sedately. "Do you know all the houses about here?"

"Just about."

"Where is A-23, 26, 475?" It was his own house, of course.

Richard looked about. "Let's see. Oh, sure, I know where it is — you see the water there?"

"Water?" Dr. Sloane made out a line of silver curving across the green.

"Sure. Real water. Just sort of running over rocks and things. It keeps running all the time. You can get across it if you step on the rocks. It's called a river."

More like a creek, thought Dr. Sloane. He had studied geography, of course, but what passed for the subject these days was really economic and cultural geography. Physical geography was almost an extinct science except among specialists. Still, he knew what rivers and creeks were, in a theoretical sort of way.

Richard was still talking. "Well, just past the river, over that hill with the big clump of trees and down the other side a way is A-23, 26, 475. It's a light green house with a white roof."

"It is?" Dr. Sloane was genuinely astonished. He hadn't known it was green.

Some small animal disturbed the grass in its anxiety to avoid the oncoming feet. Richard looked after it and shrugged. "You can't catch them. I tried."

A butterfly flitted past, a wavering bit of yellow. Dr. Sloane's eyes followed it.

There was a low hum that lay over the fields,

interspersed with an occasional harsh, calling sound, a rattle, a twittering, a chatter that rose, then fell. As his ear accustomed itself to listening, Dr. Sloane heard a thousand sounds, and none of them were manmade.

A shadow fell upon the scene, advancing toward him, covering him. It was suddenly cooler, and he looked upward, startled.

Richard said, "It's just a cloud. It'll go away in a minute — looka these flowers. They're the kind that smell."

They were several hundred yards from the Hanshaw residence. The cloud passed and the sun shone once more. Dr. Sloane looked back and was appalled at the distance they had covered. If they moved out of sight of the house and if Richard ran off, would he be able to find his way back?

He pushed the thought away impatiently and looked out toward the line of water (nearer now) and past it to where his own house must be. He thought wonderingly: Light green?

He said, "You must be quite an explorer."

Richard said, with a shy pride, "When I go to school and come back, I always try to use a different route and see new things."

"But you don't go outside every morning, do you? Sometimes you use the Doors, I imagine."

"Oh, sure."

"Why is that, Richard?" Somehow, Dr. Sloane felt there might be significance in that point.

But Richard quashed him. With his eyebrows up and a look of astonishment on his face, he said, "Well, gosh, some mornings it rains and I *have* to use the Door. I hate that, but what can you do? About two weeks ago, I got caught in the rain and I — " he looked about him automatically, and his voice sank to a whisper " — caught a cold, and wasn't Mom upset, though."

Dr. Sloane sighed. "Shall we go back now?"

There was a quick disappointment on Richards face. "Aw, what for?"

"You remind me that your mother must be waiting for us."

"I guess so." The boy turned reluctantly.

They walked slowly back. Richard was saying, chattily, "I wrote a composition at school once about how if I could go on some ancient vehicle" (he pronounced it with exaggerated care) "I'd go in a stratoliner and look at stars and clouds and things. Oh, boy, I was sure nuts."

"You'd pick something else now?"

"You bet. I'd go in an aut'm'bile, real slow. Then I'd see everything there was."

Mrs. Hanshaw seemed troubled, uncertain. "You don't think it's abnormal, then, doctor?"

"Unusual, perhaps, but not abnormal. He likes the outside."

"But how can he? It's so dirty, so unpleasant."

"That's a matter of individual taste. A hundred years ago our ancestors were all outside most of the time. Even today, I dare say there are a million Africans who have never seen a Door."

"But Richard's always been taught to behave himself the way a decent person in District A-3 is supposed to behave," said Mrs. Hanshaw, fiercely. "Not like an African or — or an ancestor."

"That may be part of the trouble, Mrs. Hanshaw. He feels this urge to go outside and yet he feels it to be wrong. He's ashamed to talk about it to you or to his teacher. It forces him into sullen retreat and it could eventually be dangerous."

"Then how can we persuade him to stop?"

Dr. Sloane said, "Don't try. Channel the activity instead. The day your Door broke down, he was forced outside, found he liked it, and that set a pattern. He used the trip to school and back as an excuse to repeat that first exciting experience. Now suppose you agree to let him out of the house for two hours on Saturdays and Sundays. Suppose he gets it through his head that after all he can go outside without necessarily having to go anywhere in the process. Don't you think he'll be willing to use the Door to go to school and back thereafter? And don't you think that will stop the trouble he's now having with his teacher and probably with his fellow pupils?"

"But then will matters remain so? Must they? Won't he ever be normal again?"

Dr. Sloane rose to his feet. "Mrs. Hanshaw, He's as normal as need be right now. Right now, he's tasting the joys of the forbidden. If you co-operate with him, show that you don't disapprove, it will lose some of its attraction right there. Then, as he grows older, he will become more aware of the expectations and demands of society. He will learn to conform. After all, there is a little of the rebel in all of us, but it generally dies down as we grow old and tired. Unless, that is, it is unreasonably suppressed and allowed to build up pressure. Don't do that. Richard will be all right."

He walked to the Door.

Mrs. Hanshaw said, "And you don't think a probe will be necessary, doctor?"

He turned and said vehemently, "No, definitely not! There is nothing about the boy that requires it. Understand? Nothing."

His fingers hesitated an inch from the combination board and the expression on his face grew lowering.

"What's the matter, Dr. Sloane?" asked Mrs. Hanshaw.

But he didn't hear her because he was thinking of the Door and the psychic probe and all the rising, choking tide of machinery. There is a little of the rebel in all of us, he thought.

So he said in a soft voice, as his hand fell away from the board and his feet turned away from the Door, "You know, it's such a beautiful day that I think I'll walk."

The Man
Who Lost The Sea

by Theodore Sturgeon

S AY YOU'RE A KID, and one dark night you're
running along the cold sand with this helicopter in your hand, saying very fast *witchy-
witchy-witchy*. You pass the sick man and he
wants you to shove off with that thing. Maybe
he thinks you're too old to play with toys. So you
squat next to him in the sand and tell him it isn't
a toy, it's a model. You tell him, "Look here, here's
something most people don't know about helicopters." You take a blade of the rotor in your
fingers and show him how it can move in the
hub, up and down a little, back and forth a little,
and twist a little, to change pitch. You start to
tell him how this flexibility does away with the
gyroscopic effect, but he won't listen. He doesn't
want to think about flying, about helicopters, or

about you, and he most especially does not want explanations about anything by anybody. Not now. Now, he wants to think about the sea. So you go away.

The sick man is buried in the cold sand with only his head and his left arm showing. He is dressed in a pressure suit and looks like a man from Mars. Built into his left sleeve is a combination timepiece and pressure gauge, the gauge with a luminous blue indicator which makes no sense, the clockhands luminous red. He can hear the pounding of surf and the soft swift pulse of his pumps. One time long ago when he was swimming he went too deep and stayed down too long and came up too fast, and when he came to, it was like this: They said, "Don't move, boy. You've got the bends. Don't even *try* to move." He had tried anyway. It hurt. So now, this time, he lies in the sand without moving, without trying.

His head isn't working right. But he knows clearly that it isn't working right, which is a strange thing that happens to people in shock sometimes. Say you were that kid, you could say how it was, because once you woke up lying in the gym office in high school and asked what had happened. They explained how you tried something on the parallel bars and fell on your head. You understand exactly, though you couldn't remember falling. Then a minute later you asked

again what had happened and they told you. You
understood it. And a minute later . . . forty-one
times they told you, and you understood. It was
just that no matter how many times they pushed
it into your head, it wouldn't stick there; but all
the while you *knew* that your head would start
working again in time. And in time it did. . . . Of
course, if you were that kid, always explaining
things to people and to yourself, you wouldn't
want to bother the sick man with it now.

Look what you've done already, making him
send you away with that angry shrug of the mind
(which, with the eyes, are the only things which
will move just now). The motionless effort costs
him a wave of nausea. He has felt seasick before
but he has never *been* seasick, and the formula
for that is to keep your eyes on the horizon and
stay busy. Now! Then he'd better get busy —
now; for there's one place especially not to be
seasick in, and that's locked up in a pressure
suit. Now!

So he busies himself as best he can, with the
seascape, landscape, sky. He lies on high ground,
his head propped on a vertical wall of black rock.
There is another such outcrop before him, whip-
topped with white sand and with smooth flat
sand. Beyond and down is valley, salt flat,
estuary; he cannot yet be sure. He is sure of the
line of footprints, which begin behind him, pass
to his left, disappear in the outcrop shadows,

and reappear beyond to vanish at last into the shadows of the valley.

Stretched across the sky is old mourning cloth, with starlight burning holes in it, and between the holes the black is absolute — wintertime, mountaintop sky-black.

(Far off on the horizon within himself he sees the swell and crest of approaching nausea; he counters with an undertow of weakness, which meets and rounds and settles the wave before it can break. Get busier. *Now.*)

Burst in on him, then, with the X-15 model. That'll get him. Hey, how about this for a gimmick? Get too high for the thin air to give you any control, you have these little jets in the wingtips, see? and on the sides of the *empennage*: bank, roll, yaw, whatever, with squirts of compressed air.

But the sick man curls his sick lip: oh, git, kid, git, will you? That has nothing to do with the sea. So you git.

Out and out the sick man forces his view, etching all he sees with a meticulous intensity, as if it might be his charge, one day, to duplicate all this. To his left is only starlit sea, windless. In front of him across the valley rounded hills with dim white epaulettes of light. To his right, the jutting corner of the black wall against which his helmet rests. (He thinks the distant moundings of nausea becalmed, but he will not look yet.

So he scans the sky, black and bright, calling Sirius, calling Pleiades, Polaris, Ursa Minor, calling that . . . that . . . Why, it *moves*. Watch it: yes, it moves! It is a fleck of light, seeming to be wrinkled, fissured rather like a chip of boiled cauliflower in the sky. (Of course, he knows better than to trust his own eyes just now.) But that movement . . .

As a child he had stood on cold sand in a frosty Cape Cod evening, watching Sputnik's steady spark rise out of the haze (madly, dawning a little north of west); and after that he had sleeplessly wound special coils for his receiver, risked his life restringing high antennas, all for the brief capture of an unreadable *tweetle-eep-tweetle* in his earphones from Vanguard, Explorer, Lunik, Discoverer, Mercury. He knew them all (well, some people collect match covers, stamps) and he knew especially that unmistakable steady sliding in the sky.

This moving fleck was a satellite; and in a moment, motionless, uninstrumented but for his chronometer and his part-brain, he will know which one. (He is grateful beyond expression — without that sliding chip of light, there were only those footprints, those wandering footprints, to tell a man he was not alone in the world.)

Say you were a kid, eager and challengeable and more than a little bright, you might in a day or so work out a way to measure the period of a satellite with nothing but a timepiece and a brain; you might eventually see that the shadow in the rocks ahead had been there from the first only because of the light from the rising satellite. Now if you check the time exactly at the moment when the shadow on the sand is equal to the height of the outcrop, and time it again when the light is at the zenith and the shadow gone, you will multiply this number of minutes by eight — think why, now: horizon to zenith is one fourth of the orbit, give or take a little, and halfway up the sky is half that quarter — and you will then know this satellite's period. You know all the periods — ninety minutes, two, two and a half hours; with that and the appearance of this bird, you'll find out which one it is.

But if you were that kid, eager or resourceful or whatever, you wouldn't jabber about it to the sick man, for not only does he not want to be bothered with you, he's thought of all that long since and is even now watching the shadows for that triangular split second of measurement. *Now!* His eyes drop to the face of his chronometer: 0400, near as makes no never mind.

He has minutes to wait now — ten? . . . thirty? . . . twenty-three? — while this baby moon eats up its slice of shadow pie; and that's too bad, the waiting, for though the inner sea is calm there are currents below, shadows that shift and swim. Be busy. Be busy. He must not swim near that great invisible amoeba, whatever happens: its first cold pseudopod is even now reaching for the vitals.

Being a knowledgeable young fellow, not quite a kid any more, wanting to help the sick man too, you want to tell him everything you know about that cold-in-the-gut, that reaching invisible surrounding implacable amoeba. You know all about it — listen, you want to yell at him, don't let that touch of cold bother you. Just know what it is, that's all. Know what it is that is touching your gut. You want to tell him, listen:

Listen, this is how you met the monster and dissected it. Listen, you were skindiving in the Grenadines, a hundred tropical shoal-water islands; you had a new blue snorkel mask, the kind with face plate and breathing tube all in one, and new blue flippers on your feet, and a new blue speargun — all this new because you'd only begun, you see; you were a beginner, aghast with pleasure at your easy intrusion into this underwater otherworld. You'd been out in a boat, you were coming back, you'd just reached the mouth of the little bay, you'd taken the notion to swim the rest of the way. You'd said as much to the boys and slipped into the warm silky water. You brought your gun.

Not far to go at all, but then beginners find wet distances deceiving. For the first five minutes or so it was delightful, the sun hot on your back and the water so warm it seemed not to have any temperature at all and you were flying. With your face under the water, your mask was not so much attached as part of you, your wide blue flippers trod away yards, your gun rode all but weightless in your hand, the taut rubber sling making an occasional hum as your passage plucked it in the sunlit green. In your ears the breathy monotone of the snorkel tube crooned, and through the invisible disk of plate glass you saw wonders. The bay was shallow — ten, twelve feet or so — and sandy, with great growths of brain-, bone-, and fire-coral, intricate waving sea fans, and fish — such fish! Scarlet and green and aching azure, gold and rose and slate color studded with sparks of enamel blue, pink and peach and silver. And that *thing* got into you, that ... monster.

There were enemies in this otherworld: the sand-colored spotted sea snake with his big ugly head and turned-down mouth who would not retreat but lay watching the intruder pass; and the mottled moray with jaws like bolt cutters; and somewhere around, certainly, the barracuda with his undershot face and teeth turned inward so that he must take away whatever he might strike. There were urchins — the plump white sea egg with its thick fur of sharp quills and the black ones with the long slender spines that would break off in unwary flesh and fester there for weeks; and filefish and stonefish with their poisoned barbs and lethal meat; and the stingaree who could drive his spike through a leg bone. Yet these were not *monsters*, and could not matter to you, the invader churning along above them all. For you were above them in so many ways — armed, rational, comforted by the close shore (ahead the beach, the rocks on each side) and by the presence of the boat not too far behind. Yet you were attacked.

At first it was uneasiness, not pressing, but pervasive, a contact quite as intimate as that of the sea; you were sheathed in it. And also there was the touch — the cold inward contact. Aware of it at last, you laughed: for Pete's sake, what's there to be scared of?

The monster, the amoeba.

You raised your head and looked back in air. The boat had edged in to the cliff at the right; someone was giving a last poke around for lobster. You waved at the boat; it was your gun you waved, and emerging from the water it gained its latent ounces so that you sank a bit, and as if you had no snorkel on, you tipped your head back to get a breath. But tipping your head back plunged the end of the tube under water; the valve closed; you drew in a hard lungful of nothing at all. You dropped your face under; up came the tube; you got your air, and along with it a bullet of seawater which struck you somewhere inside the throat. You coughed it out and floundered, sobbing as you sucked in air, inflating your chest until it hurt, and the air you got seemed no good, no good at all, worthless devitalized inert gas.

You clenched your teeth and headed for the beach, kicking strongly and knowing it was the right thing to do; and then below and to the right you saw a great bulk mounding up out of the sand floor of the sea. You knew it was only the reef, rocks and coral and weed, but the sight of it made you scream; you didn't care what you knew. You turned hard left to avoid it, fought by as if it would reach for you, and you couldn't get air, couldn't get air, for all the unobstructed hooting of your snorkel tube. You couldn't bear the mask suddenly, not for another second, so you shoved it upward clear of your mouth and rolled over, floating on your back and opening your mouth to the sky and breathing with a sort of quacking noise.

It was then and there that the monster well and truly engulfed you, mantling you round and about within itself — formless, borderless, the illimitable amoeba. The beach, mere yards away, and the rocky arms of the bay, and the not-too-distant boat — these you could identify but no longer distinguish, for they were all one and the same thing . . . the thing called unreachable.

You fought that way for a time, on your back,

dangling the gun under and behind you and straining to get enough warm sun-stained air into your chest. And in time some particles of sanity began to swirl in the roil of your mind, and to dissolve and tint it. The air pumping in and out of your square-grinned frightened mouth began to be meaningful at last, and the monster relaxed away from you.

You took stock, saw surf, beach, a leaning tree. You felt the new scend of your body as the rollers humped to become breakers. Only a dozen firm kicks brought you to where you could roll over and double up; your shin struck coral with a lovely agony and you stood in foam and waded ashore. You gained the wet sand, hard sand, and ultimately with two more paces powered by bravado, you crossed high-water mark and lay in the dry sand, unable to move.

You lay in the sand, and before you were able to move or to think, you were able to feel a triumph — a triumph because you were alive and knew that much without thinking at all.

When you *were* able to think, your first thought was of the gun, and the first move you were able to make was to let go at last of the thing. You had nearly died because you had not let it go before; without it you would not have been burdened and you would not have panicked. You had (you began to understand) kept it because someone else would have had to retrieve it —

easily enough — and you could not have stood the laughter. You had almost died because they might laugh at you.

This was the beginning of the dissection, analysis, study of the monster. It began then; it had never finished. Some of what you had learned from it was merely important; some of the rest — vital.

You had learned, for example, never to swim farther with a snorkel than you could swim back without one. You learned never to burden yourself with the unnecessary in an emergency: even a hand or a foot might be as expendable as a gun; pride was expendable, dignity was. You learned never to dive alone, even if they laugh at you, even if you have to shoot a fish yourself and say afterwards "we" shot it. Most of all, you learned that fear has many fingers, and one of them — a simple one, made of two great a concentration of carbon dioxide in your blood, as from too-rapid breathing in and out of the same tube — is not really fear at all but feels like fear, and can turn into panic and kill you.

Listen, you want to say, listen, there isn't anything wrong with such an experience or with all the study it leads to, because a man who can learn enough from it could become fit enough, cautious enough, foresighted, unafraid, modest, teachable enough to be chosen, to be qualified for . . .

You lose the thought, or turn it away, because the sick man feels that cold touch deep inside, feels it right now, feels it beyond ignoring, above and beyond anything that you, with all your experience and certainty, could explain to him even if he would listen, which he won't. Make him, then; tell him the cold touch is some simple explainable thing like anoxemia, like gladness even; some triumph that he will be able to appreciate when his head is working right again.

Triumph? Here he's alive after . . . whatever it is, and that doesn't seem to be triumph enough, though it was in the Grenadines, and that other time, when he got the bends, saved his own life, saved two other lives. Now, somehow, it's not the same: there seems to be a reason why just being alive afterwards isn't a triumph.

Why not triumph? Because not twelve, not twenty, not even thirty minutes is it taking the satellite to complete its eighth-of-an-orbit: fifty minutes are gone, and still there's a slice of shadow yonder. It is this, *this* which is placing the cold finger upon his heart, and he doesn't know why, he doesn't know why, he *will* not know why; he is afraid he shall when his head is working again. . . .

Oh, where's the kid? Where is any way to busy the mind, apply it to something, anything else but the watch hand which outruns the moon? Here, kid: come over here — what you got there?

If you were the kid, then you'd forgive everything and hunker down with your new model, not a toy, not a helicopter or a rocket-plane, but the big one, the one that looks like an overgrown cartridge. It's so big even as a model that even an angry sick man wouldn't call it a toy. A giant cartridge, but watch: the lower four fifths is Alpha — all muscle — over a million pounds thrust. (Snap it off, throw it away.) Half the rest is Beta — all brains — it puts you on your way. (Snap it off, throw it away.) And now look at the polished fraction which is left. Touch a control somewhere and see — see? It has wings — wide triangular wings. This is Gamma, the one with wings, and on its back is a small sausage; it is a moth with a sausage on its back. The sausage (click! it comes free) is Delta. Delta is the last, the smallest: Delta is the way home.

What will they think of next? Quite a toy. Quite a toy. Beat it, kid. The satellite is almost overhead, the sliver of shadow going . . . going . . . almost gone and . . . gone.

Check: 0459. Fifty-nine minutes? give or take a few. Times eight . . . 472 . . . is, uh, 7 hours 52 minutes.

Seven hours fifty-two minutes? Why there isn't a satellite round earth with a period like that. In all the solar system there's only . . .

The cold finger turns fierce, implacable.

The east is paling and the sick man turns to it,

wanting the light, the sun, an end to questions
whose answers couldn't be looked upon. The sea
stretches endlessly out to the growing light, and
endlessly, somewhere out of sight, the surf roars.
The paling east bleaches the sandy hilltops and
throws the line of footprints into aching relief.
That would be the buddy, the sick man knows,
gone for help. He cannot at the moment recall
who the buddy is, but in time he will, and meanwhile the footprints make him less alone.

The sun's upper rim thrusts itself above the
horizon with a flash of green, instantly gone. There
is no dawn, just the green flash and then a clear
white blast of unequivocal sunup. The sea could
not be whiter, more still, if it were frozen and
snow-blanketed. In the west, stars still blaze, and
overhead the crinkled satellite is scarcely
abashed by the growing light. A formless jumble
in the valley below begins to resolve itself into a
sort of tent city, or installation of some kind,
with tubelike and saillike buildings. This would
have meaning for the sick man if his head were
working right. Soon, it would. Will. (Oh . . .)

The sea, out on the horizon just under the rising
sun, is behaving strangely, for in that place
where properly belongs a pool of unbearable
brightness, there is instead a notch of brown. It
is as if the white fire of the sun is drinking dry
the sea — for look, look! the notch becomes a
bow and the bow a crescent, racing ahead of the

sunlight, white sea ahead of it and behind it a cocoa-dry stain spreading across and down toward where he watches.

Beside the finger of fear which lies on him, another finger places itself, and another, making ready for that clutch, that grip, that ultimate insane squeeze of panic. Yet beyond that again, past that squeeze when it comes, to be savored if the squeeze is only fear and not panic, lies triumph — triumph and a glory. It is perhaps this which constitutes his whole battle: to fit himself, prepare himself to bear the utmost that fear could do, for if he can do that, there is a triumph on the other side. But . . . not yet. Please, not yet awhile.

Something flies (or flew, or will fly — he is a little confused on this point) toward him, from the far right where the stars still shine. It is not a bird and it is unlike any aircraft on earth, for the aerodynamics are wrong. Wings so wide and so fragile would be useless, would melt and tear away in any of Earth's atmosphere but the outer fringes. He sees then (because he prefers to see it so) that it is the kid's model, or part of it, and for a toy, it does very well indeed.

It is the part called Gamma, and it glides in, balancing, parallels the sand and holds away, holds away slowing, then settles, all in slow motion, throwing up graceful sheet fountains of fine sand from its skids. And it runs along the ground for an impossible distance, letting down its weight by the ounce and stingily the ounce, until *look out* until a skid *look out* fits itself into a bridged crevasse *look out, look out!* and still moving on, it settles down to the struts. Gamma then, tired, digs her wide left wingtip carefully into the racing sand, digs it in hard; and as the wing breaks off, Gamma slews, sidles, slides slowly, pointing her other triangular tentlike wing at the sky, and broadside crushes into the rocks at the valley's end.

As she rolls smashing over, there breaks from her broad back the sausage, the little Delta, which somersaults away to break its back upon the rocks, and through the broken hull spill smashed shards of graphite from the moderator of her powerpile. *Look out! Look out!* and at the same instant from the finally checked mass of Gamma there explodes a doll, which slides and tumbles into the sand, into the rocks and smashed hot graphite from the wreck of Delta.

The sick man numbly watches this toy destroy itself: what will they think of next — and with a gelid horror prays at the doll lying in the raging rubble of the atomic pile; *don't stay there, man — get away! get away! that's hot, you know?* But it seems like a night and a day and half another night before the doll staggers to its feet and, clumsy in its pressure suit, runs away up the valleyside, climbs a sand-topped outcrop, slips, falls, lies under a slow cascade of cold ancient sand until, but for an arm and the helmet, it is buried.

The sun is high now, high enough to show the sea is not a sea, but brown plain with the frost burned off it, as now it burns away from the hills, diffusing in air and blurring the edges of the sun's disk, so that in a very few minutes there is no sun at all, but only a glare in the east. Then the valley below loses its shadows, and like an arrangement in a diorama, reveals the form and nature of the wreckage below: no tent city this, no installation, but the true real ruin of Gamma and the eviscerated hulk of Delta. (Alpha was the muscle, Beta the brain; Gamma was a bird, but Delta, Delta was the way home.

And from it stretches the line of footprints, to and by the sick man, above to the bluff, and gone with the sandslide which had buried him there. Whose footprints?

He knows whose, whether or not he knows that he knows, or wants to or not. He knows what satellite has (give or take a bit) a period like that. (Want it exactly? It's 7.66 hours.) He knows what world has such a night, and such a frosty glare by day. He knows these things as he knows how spilled radioactives will pour the crash and mutter of surf into a man's earphones.

Say you were that kid: say, instead, at last, that you are the sick man, for they are the same; surely then you can understand why of all things, even while shattered, shocked, sick with radiation calculated (leaving), radiation computed (arriving), and radiation past all bearing (lying in the wreckage of Delta), you would want to think of the sea. For no farmer who fingers the soil with love and knowledge, no poet who sings of it, artist, contractor, engineer, even child bursting into tears at the inexpressible beauty of a field of daffodils — none of these is as intimate with Earth as those who live on, live with, breathe and drift in its seas. So of these things you must think; with these you must dwell until you are less sick and more ready to face the truth.

The truth, then, is that the satellite fading here is Phobos, that those footprints are your own, that there is no sea here, that you have crashed and are killed and will in a moment be dead. The cold hand ready to squeeze and still your heart is not anoxia or even fear, it is death. Now, if there is something more important than this, now is the time for it to show itself.

The sick man looks at the line of his own footprints, which testify that he is alone, and at the wreckage below, which states that there is no way back, and at the white east and the mottled west and the paling black satellite above. Surf sounds in his ears. He hears his pumps. He hears what is left of his breathing. The cold clamps down and folds him round past measuring, past all limits.

Then he speaks, cries out: then with joy he takes his triumph at the other side of death, as one takes a great fish, as one completes a skilled and mighty task, rebalances at the end of some great daring leap; and as he used to say, "We shot a fish" he uses no "I":

"God," he cries, dying on Mars, "God, we made it!"

Phoenix

by Clark Ashton Smith

RODIS AND HILAR had climbed from their natal caverns to the top chamber of the high observatory tower. Pressed close together, for warmth as well as love, they stood at an eastern window looking forth on hills and valleys dim with perennial starlight. They had come up to watch the rising of the sun: that sun which they had never seen except as an orb of blackness, occluding the zodiacal stars in its course from horizon to horizon.

Thus their ancestors had seen it for millenniums. By some freak of cosmic law, unforeseen, and inexplicable to astronomers and physicists, the sun's cooling had been comparatively sudden, and the Earth had not suffered the long-drawn complete desiccation of such planets as Mercury and Mars. Rivers, lakes, seas, had frozen solid; and the air itself had congealed, all in a term of years historic rather than geologic. Millions of the Earth's inhabitants had perished, trapped by the glacial ice, the centigrade cold. The rest, armed with all the resources of science, had found time to entrench themselves against the cosmic night in a world of ramified caverns, dug by atomic excavators far below the surface.

Here, by the light of artificial orbs, and the heat drawn from the planet's still-molten depths, life went on much as it had done in the outer world. Trees, fruits, grasses, grains, vegetables, were grown in isotope-stimulated soil or hydroponic gardens, affording food, renewing a breathable atmosphere. Domestic animals were kept, birds flew, and insects crawled or fluttered. The rays considered necessary for life and health were afforded by the sun-bright lamps that shone eternally in all the caverns.

Little of the old science was lost; but, on the other hand, there was now little advance. Existence had become the conserving of a fire menaced by inexorable night. Generation by generation a mysterious sterility had lessened the numbers of the race from millions to a few thousands. As time went on, a similar sterility began to affect animals; even plants no longer flourished with their first abundance. No biologist could determine the cause with certainty.

Perhaps man, as well as other terrestrial life forms, was past his prime, and had begun to undergo collectively the inevitable senility that comes to the individual. Or perhaps, having been a surface dweller throughout most of his evolution, he was inadaptable to the cribbed and prisoned life, the caverned light and air, and was dying slowly from the deprivation of things he had almost forgotten.

Indeed, the world that had once flourished beneath a living sun was little more than a legend now, a tradition preserved by art and literature and history. Its beetling Babelian cities, its fecund hills and plains, were swathed impenetrably in snow and ice and solidified air. No living man had gazed upon it, except from the night-bound towers maintained as observatories.

Still, however, the dreams of men were often lit by primordial memories, in which the sun shone on rippling waters and waving trees and grass. And their waking hours were sometimes touched by an undying nostalgia for the lost earth. . . .

Alarmed by the prospect of racial extinction, the most able and brilliant savants had conceived a project that was seemingly no less desperate than fantastic. The plan, if executed, might lead to failure or even to the planet's destruction. But all the necessary steps had now been taken toward its launching.

It was of this plan that Rodis and Hilar spoke, standing clasped in each other's arms, as they waited for the rising of the dead sun.

"And you must go?" said Rodis, with averted eyes and voice that quavered a little.

"Of course. It is a duty and an honor. I am regarded as the foremost of the younger atomicists. The actual placing and timing of the bombs will devolve largely upon me."

"But — are you sure of success? There are so many risks, Hilar." The girl shuddered, clasping her lover with convulsive tightness.

"We are not sure of anything," Hilar admitted. "But, granting that our calculations are correct, the multiple charges of fissionable materials, including more than half the solar elements, should start chain reactions that will restore the sun to its former incandescence. Of course, the explosion may be too sudden and too violent, involving the nearer planets in the formation of a nova. But we do not believe that this will happen — since an explosion of such magnitude would require instant disruption of *all* the sun's elements. Such disruption should not occur without a starter for each separate atomic structure. Science has never been able to break down all the known elements. If it had been, Earth itself would undoubtedly have suffered destruction in the old atomic wars."

Hilar paused, and his eyes dilated, kindling with a visionary fire.

"How glorious," he went on, "to use for a purpose of cosmic renovation the deadly projectiles designed by our forefathers only to blast and destroy. Stored in sealed caverns, they have not been used since men abandoned the Earth's surface so many millenniums ago. Nor have the old spaceships been used either. . . . An interstellar drive was never perfected; and our voyagings were always limited to the other worlds of our own system — none of which was inhabited, or inhabitable. Since the sun's cooling and darkening, there had been no object in visiting any of them. But the ships too were stored away. And the newest and speediest one, powered with antigravity magnets, has been made ready for our voyage to the sun."

Rodis listened silently, with an awe that seemed to have subdued her misgivings, while Hilar continued to speak of the tremendous project upon which he, with six other chosen technicians, was about to embark. In the meanwhile, the black sun rose slowly into heavens thronged with the cold ironic blazing of innumerable stars, among which no planet shone. It blotted out the sting of the Scorpion, poised at that hour above the eastern hills. It was smaller but nearer than the igneous orb of history and legend. In its center, like a Cyclopean eye, there burned a single spot of dusty red fire, believed to mark the eruption of some immense volcano amid the measureless and cinder-blackened landscape.

To one standing in the icebound valley below the observatory, it would have seemed that the tower's lighted window was a yellow eye that stared back from the dead Earth to that crimson eye of the dead sun.

"Soon," said Hilar, "you will climb to this chamber — and see the morning that none has seen for a century of centuries. The thick ice will thaw from the peaks and valleys, running in streams to re-molten lakes and oceans. The liquefied air will rise in clouds and vapors, touched with the spectrum-tinted splendor of the light. Again, across Earth, will blow the winds of the four quarters; and grass and flowers will grow, and trees burgeon from tiny saplings. And man, the dweller in closed caves and abysses, will return to his proper heritage."

"How wonderful it all sounds," murmured Rodis. "But . . . you will come back to me?"

"I will come back to you . . . in the sunlight," said Hilar.

The space vessel *Phosphor* lay in a huge cavern beneath that region which had once been known as the Atlas Mountains. The cavern's mile-thick roof had been partly blasted away by atomic disintegrators. A great circlar shaft slanted upward to the surface, forming a mouth in the mountainside through which the stars of the Zodiac were visible. The prow of the *Phospor* pointed at the stars.

All was now ready for its launching. A score of dignitaries and savants, looking like strange ungainly monsters in suits and helmets worn against the spatial cold that had invaded the cavern, were present for the occasion. Hilar and his six companions had already gone aboard the *Phosphor* and had closed its airlocks.

Inscrutable and silent behind their metalloid helmets, the watchers waited. There was no ceremony, no speaking or waving of farewells; nothing to indicate that a world's destiny depended on the mission of the vessel.

Like mouths of fire-belching dragons the stern rockets flared, and the *Phosphor*, like a wingless bird, soared upward through the great shaft and vanished.

Hilar, gazing through a rear port, saw for a few moments the lamp-bright window of that tower in which he had stood so recently with Rodis. The window was a golden spark that swirled downward in abysses of devouring night — and was extinguished. Behind it, he knew, his beloved stood watching the *Phosphor*'s departure. It was a symbol, he mused . . . a symbol of life, of memory . . . of the suns themselves . . . of all things that flash briefly and fall into oblivion.

But such thoughts, he felt, should be dismissed. They were unworthy of one whom his fellows had appointed as a light-bringer, a Prometheus who should rekindle the dead sun and re-lumine the dark world.

There were no days, only hours of eternal starlight, to measure the time in which they sped outward through the void. The rockets, used for initial propulsion, no longer flamed astern; and the vessel flew in darkness, except for the gleaming Argus eyes of its ports, drawn now by the mighty gravitational drag of the blind sun.

Test flights had been considered unnecessary for the *Phosphor*. All its machinery was in perfect condition; and the mechanics involved were simple and easily mastered. None of its crew had ever been in extraterrestrial space before; but all were well-trained in astronomy, mathematics, and the various techniques essential to a voyage between worlds. There were two navigators; one rocket engineer; and two engineers who would operate the powerful generators, charged with a negative magnetism reverse to that of gravity, with which they hoped to approach, circumnavigate, and eventually depart in safety from an orb enormously heavier than the system's nine planets merged into one. Hilar and his assistant, Han Joas, completed the personnel. Their sole task was the timing, landing, and distribution of the bombs.

All were descendants of a mixed race of Latin, Semitic, Hamitic, and Negroid ancestry: a race that had dwelt, before the sun's cooling, in countries south of the Mediterranean, where the former deserts had been rendered fertile by a vast irrigation system of lakes and canals.

This mixture, after so many centuries of cavern life, had produced a characteristically slender, well-knit type, of short or medium stature and pale olive complexion.

To a surprising extent, in view of the vast intermediate eras of historic and geographic change, this people had preserved many preatomic traditions and even something of the old classic Mediterranean cultures. Their language bore distinct traces of Latin, Greek, Spanish, and Arabic.

Remnants of other peoples, those of subequatorial Asia and America, had survived the universal glaciation by burrowing underground. Radio communication had been maintained with these peoples till within fairly recent times, and had then ceased. It was believed that they had died out, or had retrograded into savagery, losing the civilization to which they had once attained.

Hour after hour, the *Phosphor* sped onward through the black unvarying void. To Hilar, it seemed at times that they flew merely through a darker and vaster cavern whose remote walls were spangled by the stars as if by radiant orbs.

He had thought to feel the overwhelming vertigo of unbottomed and undirectioned space. Instead, there was a weird sense of circumscription by the ambient night and emptiness, together with a sense of cyclic repetition, as if all that was happening had happened many times before and must recur often through endless future kalpas.

Had he and his companions gone forth in former cycles to the relighting of former perished suns? Would they go forth again, to rekindle suns that would flame and die in some posterior universe? Had there always been, would there always be, a Rodis who awaited his return?

Of these thoughts he spoke only to Han Joas, who shared something of his innate mysticism and his trend toward cosmic speculation. But mostly the two talked of the mysteries of the atom and its typhonic powers, and discussed the problems with which they would shortly be confronted.

The ship carried several hundred disruption bombs, many of untried potency: the unused heritage of ancient wars that had left chasm scars and lethal radioactive areas, some a thousand miles or more in extent, for the planetary glaciers to cover. There were bombs of iron, calcium, sodium, helium, hydrogen, sulphur, potassium, magnesium, copper, chromium, strontium, barium, zinc: elements that had all been anciently revealed in the solar spectrum. Even at the apex of their madness, the warring nations had wisely refrained from employing more than a few such bombs at any one time. Chain reactions had sometimes been started; but, fortunately, had died out.

Hilar and Han Joas hoped to distribute the bombs at intervals over the sun's entire circumference; preferably in large deposits of the same elements as those of which they were composed. The vessel was equipped with radar apparatus by which the various elements could be detected and located. The bombs would be timed to explode with as much simultaneity as possible. If all went well, the *Phosphor* would have fulfilled its mission and traveled most of the return distance to Earth before the explosions occurred.

It had been conjectured that the sun's interior was composed of still-molten magma, covered by a relatively thin crust: a seething flux of matter that manifested itself in volcanic activities. Only one of the volcanoes was visible from Earth to the naked eye; but numerous others had been revealed by telescopic study. Now, as the *Phosphor* drew near to its destination, these others flamed out on the huge, slowly rotating orb that had darkened a fourth of the ecliptic and had blotted Libra, Scorpio, and Sagittarius wholly from view.

For a long time it had seemed to hang above the voyagers. Now, suddenly, as if through some prodigious legerdemain, it lay beneath them: a monstrous, ever-broadening disk of ebon, eyed with fiery craters, veined and spotted and blotched with unknown pallid radioactives. It was like the buckler of some macrocosmic giant of the night, who had entrenched himself in the abyss lying between the worlds.

The *Phosphor* plunged toward it like a steel splinter drawn by some tremendous lodestone.

Each member of the crew had been trained beforehand for the part he was to play; and everything had been timed with the utmost precision. Sybal and Samac, the engineers of the antigravity magnets, began to manipulate the switches that would build up resistance to the solar drag. The generators, bulking to the height of three men, with induction coils that suggested some colossal Laocoon, could draw from cosmic space a negative force capable of counteracting many Earth gravities. In past ages they had defied easily the pull of Jupiter; and the ship had even coasted as near to the blazing sun as its insulation and refrigeration systems would safely permit. Therefore it seemed reasonable to expect that the voyagers could accomplish their purpose of approaching closely to the darkened globe, of circling it, and pulling away when the disruption charges had all been planted.

A dull, subsonic vibration, felt rather than heard, began to emanate from the magnets. It shook the vessel, ached in the voyagers' tissues. Intently, with anxiety unbetrayed by their impassive features, they watched the slow, gradual building-up of power shown by gauge dials on which giant needles crept like horologic hands, registering the reversed gravities one after one, till a drag equivalent to that of fifteen Earths had been neutralized. The clamp of the solar gravitation, drawing them on with projectilelike velocity, crushing them to their seats with relentless increase of weight, was loosened. The needles crept on . . . more slowly now . . . to sixteen . . . to seventeen . . . and stopped. The *Phosphor*'s fall had been retarded but not arrested. And the switches stood at their last notch.

Sybal spoke, in answer to the unuttered questions of his companions.

"Something is wrong. Perhaps there has been some unforeseen deterioration of the coils, in whose composition strange and complex alloys were used. Some of the elements may have been unstable — or have developed instability through age. Or perhaps there is some interfering unknown force, born of the sun's decay. At any rate, it is impossible to build more power toward the twenty-seven antigravities we will require close to the solar surface."

Samac added: "The decelerative jets will increase our resistance to nineteen antigravities. It will still be far from enough, even at our present distance."

"How much time have we?" inquired Hilar, turning to the navigators, Calaf and Caramond.

The two conferred and calculated.

"By using the decelerative jets, it will be two hours before we reach the sun," announced Calaf finally.

As if his announcement had been an order, Eibano, the jet engineer, promptly jerked the levers that fired to full power the reversing rockets banked in the *Phosphor*'s nose and sides. There was a slight further deceleration of their descent, a further lightening of the grievous weight that oppressed them. But the *Phosphor* still plunged irreversibly sunward.

Hilar and Han Joas exchanged a glance of understanding and agreement. They rose stiffly from their seats, and moved heavily toward the magazine, occupying fully half the ship's interior, in which the hundreds of disruption bombs were racked. It was unnecessary to announce their purpose; and no one spoke either in approval or demur.

Hilar opened the magazine's door; and he and Han Joas paused on the threshold, looking back. They saw for the last time the faces of their fellow-voyagers, expressing no other emotion than resignation, vignetted, as it were, on the verge of destruction. Then they entered the magazine, closing its door behind them.

They set to work methodically, moving back to back along a narrow aisle between the racks in which the immense ovoid bombs were piled in

strict order according to their respective elements.
Because of the various coordinated dials and
switches involved, it was a matter of minutes to
prepare a single bomb for the explosion. Therefore, Hilar and Han Joas, in the time at their disposal, could do no more than set the timing and
detonating mechanism of one bomb of each element. A great chronometer, ticking at the magazine's farther end, enabled them to accomplish
this task with precision. The bombs were thus
timed to explode simultaneously, detonating the
others through chain reaction, at the moment
when the *Phosphor* should touch the sun's surface.

The solar pull, strengthening as the *Phosphor*
fell to its doom, had now made their movements
slow and difficult. It would, they feared, immo-
bilize them before they could finish preparing a
second series of bombs for detonation. Laboriously, beneath the burden of a weight already tre-
bled, they made their way to seats that faced a
reflector in which the external cosmos was imaged.

It was an awesome and stupendous scene on
which they gazed. The sun's globe had broadened
vastly, filling the nether heavens. Half-seen, a dim
unhorizoned landscape, fitfully lit by the crimson
far-sundered flares of volcanoes, by bluish zones
and patches of strange radioactive minerals, it
deepened beneath them abysmally, disclosing
mountains that would have made the Himalayas

seem like hillocks, revealing chasms that might have engulfed asteroids and planets.

At the center of this Cyclopean landscape burned the great volcano that had been called Hephaestus by astronomers. It was the same volcano watched by Hilar and Rodis from the observatory window. Tongues of flame a hundred miles in length arose and licked skyward from a crater that seemed the mouth of some ultramundane hell.

Hilar and Han Joas no longer heard the chronometer's portentous ticking, and had no eyes for the watching of its ominous hands. Such watching was needless now: there was nothing more to be done, and nothing before them but eternity. They measured their descent by the broadening of the dim solar plain, the leaping into salience of new mountains, the deepening of new chasms and gulfs in the globe that had now lost all semblance of a sphere.

It was plain now that the *Phosphor* would fall directly into the flaming and yawning crater of Hephaestus. Faster and faster it plunged, heavier grew the piled chains of gravity that giants could not have lifted. . . .

At the very last, the reflector on which Hilar and Han Joas peered was filled entirely by the tongued volcanic fires that enveloped the *Phosphor*.

Then, without eyes to see or ears to apprehend,

they were part of the pyre from which the sun,
like a Phoenix, was reborn.

Rodis, climbing to the tower, after a period of
fitful sleep and troublous dreams, saw from its
window the rising of the rekindled orb.

It dazzled her, though its glory was half
dimmed by rainbow-colored mists that fumed
from the icy mountaintops. It was a sight filled
with marvel and with portent. Thin rills of downward threading water had already begun to fret
the glacial armor on slopes and scarps; and later
they would swell to cataracts, laying bare the
buried soil and stone. Vapors, that seemed to flow
and fluctuate on renascent winds, swam sunward
from lakes of congealed air at the valley's bottom.
It was a visible resumption of the elemental life
and activity so long suspended in hibernal night.
Even through the tower's insulating walls, Rodis
felt the solar warmth that later would awaken the
seeds and spores of plants that had lain dormant
for cycles.

Her heart was stirred to wonder by the spec-
tacle. But beneath the wonder was a great numb-
ness and a sadness like unmelting ice. Hilar, she
knew, would never return to her — except as a
ray of the light, a spark of the vital heat, that he
had helped to relumine. For the nonce, there was
irony rather than comfort in the memory of his
promise: "I will come back to you — in the sunlight."

Third From The Sun

by Richard Matheson

His eyes were open five seconds before the alarm was to go off. There was no effort in waking. It was sudden. Coldly conscious, he reached out his left hand in the dark and pushed in the stop. The alarm glowed a second, then faded.

At his side, his wife put her hand on his arm.

"Did you sleep?" he asked.

"No, did you?"

"A little," he said. "Not much."

She was silent for a few seconds. He heard her throat contract. She shivered. He knew what she was going to say.

"We're still going?" she asked.

He twisted his shoulders on the bed and took a deep breath.

"Yes," he said, and he felt her fingers tighten on his arm.

"What time is it?" she asked.

"About five."

"We'd better get ready."

"Yes, we'd better."

They made no move.

"You're sure we can get on the ship without anyone noticing?" she asked.

"They think it's just another test flight. Nobody will be checking."

She didn't say anything. She moved a little closer to him. He felt how cold her skin was.

"I'm afraid," she said.

He took her hand and held it in a tight grip. "Don't be," he said. "We'll be safe."

"It's the children I'm worried about."

"We'll be safe," he repeated.

She lifted his hand to her lips and kissed it gently.

"All right," she said.

They both sat up in the darkness. He heard her stand. Her night garment rustled to the floor. She didn't pick it up. She stood still, shivering in the cold morning air.

"You're sure we don't need anything else with us?" she asked.

"No, nothing. I have all the supplies we need in the ship. Anyway . . ."

"What?"

"We can't carry anything past the guard," he said. "He has to think you and the kids are just coming to see me off."

She began dressing. He threw off the covering and got up. He went across the cold floor to the closet and dressed.

"I'll get the children up," she said.

He grunted, pulling clothes over his head. At the door she stopped. "Are you sure . . ." she began.

"What?"

"Won't the guard think it's funny that . . . that our neighbors are coming down to see you off, too?"

He sank down on the bed and fumbled for the clasps on his shoes.

"We'll have to take that chance," he said. "We need them with us."

She sighed. "It seems so cold. So calculating."

He straightened up and saw her silhouette in the doorway.

"What else can we do?" he asked intensely. "We can't interbreed our own children."

"No," she said. "It's just . . ."

"Just what?"

"Nothing, darling. I'm sorry."

She closed the door. Her footsteps disappeared down the hall. The door to the children's room opened. He heard their two voices. A cheerless smile raised his lips. You'd think it was a holiday, he thought.

He pulled on his shoes. At least the kids didn't know what was happening. They thought they were going to take him down to the field. They thought they'd come back and tell all their schoolmates about it. They didn't know they'd never come back.

He finished clasping his shoes and stood up. He shuffled over to the bureau and turned on the light. It was odd, such an undistinguished looking man planning this.

Cold. Calculating. Her words filled his mind again. Well, there was no other way. In a few years, probably less, the whole planet would go up with a blinding flash. This was the only way out. Escaping, starting all over again with a few people on a new planet.

He stared at the reflection.

"There's no other way," he said.

He glanced around the bedroom. Good-bye this part of my life. Turning off the lamp was like turning off a light in his mind. He closed the door gently behind him and slid his fingers off the worn handle.

His son and daughter were going down the ramp. They were talking in mysterious whispers. He shook his head in slight amusement.

His wife waited for him. They went down together, holding hands.

"I'm not afraid, darling," she said. "It'll be all right."

"Sure," he said. "Sure it will."

They all went in to eat. He sat down with his children. His wife poured out juice for them. Then she went to get the food.

"Help your mother, doll," he told his daughter. She got up.

"Pretty soon, haah, pop?" his son said. "Pretty soon, haah?"

"Take it easy," he cautioned. "Remember what I told you. If you say a word of it to anybody I'll have to leave you behind."

A dish shattered on the floor. He darted a glance at his wife. She was staring at him, her lips trembling.

She averted her eyes and bent down. She fumbled at the pieces, picked up a few. Then she dropped them all, stood up, and pushed them against the wall with her shoe.

"As if it mattered," she said nervously. "As if it mattered whether the place is clean or not."

The children were watching her in surprise.

"What is it?" asked the daughter.

"Nothing, darling, nothing," she said. "I'm just nervous. Go back to the table. Drink your juice. We have to eat quickly. The neighbors will be here soon."

"Pop, why are the neighbors coming with us?" asked his son.

"Because," he said vaguely, "they want to. Now forget it. Don't talk about it so much."

The room was quiet. His wife brought their food and set it down. Only her footsteps broke the silence. The children kept glancing at each other, at their father. He kept his eyes on the plate. The food tasted flat and thick in his mouth and he felt his heart thudding against the wall of his chest. Last day. This is the last day.

"You'd better eat," he told his wife.

She sat down to eat. As she lifted the eating utensil the door buzzer sounded. The utensil skidded out of her nerveless fingers and clattered on the floor. He reached out quickly and put his hand on hers.

"All right, darling," he said. "It's all right. He turned to the children. "Go answer the door," he told them.

"Both of us?" his daughter asked.

"Both of you."

"But . . ."

"Do as I say."

They slid off their chairs and left the room, glancing back at their parents.

When the sliding door shut off their view, he turned back to his wife. Her face was pale and tight; she had her lips pressed together.

"Darling, please," he said. "Please. You know I wouldn't take you if I wasn't sure it was safe. You know how many times I've flown the ship before.

And I know just where we're going. It's safe. Believe me it's safe."

She pressed his hand against her cheek. She closed her eyes and large tears ran out under her lids and down her cheeks.

"It's not that so m-much," she said. "It's just ... leaving, never coming back. We've been here all our lives. It isn't like ... like moving. We can't come back. Ever."

"Listen, darling," his voice was tense and hurried. "You know as well as I do. In a matter of years, maybe less, there's going to be another war, a terrible one. There won't be a thing left. We have to leave. For our children, for ourselves ..."

He paused, testing the words in his mind.

"For the future of life itself," he finished weakly. He was sorry he said it. Early in the morning over prosaic food, that kind of talk didn't sound right. Even if it was true.

"Just don't be afraid," he said. "We'll be all right."

She squeezed his hand.

"I know," she said quietly. "I know."

There were footsteps coming toward them. He pulled out a tissue and gave it to her. She hastily dabbed at her face.

The door slid open. The neighbors and their son and daughter came in. The children were excited. They had trouble keeping it down.

"Good-morning," the neighbor said.

The neighbor's wife went to his wife and the two of them went over to the window and talked in low voices. The children stood around, fidgeted, and looked nervously at each other.

"You've eaten?" he asked his neighbor.

"Yes," his neighbor said. "Don't you think we'd better be going?"

"I suppose so," he said.

They left all the dishes on the table. His wife went upstairs and got garments for the family.

He and his wife stayed on the porch a moment while the rest went out to the ground car.

"Should we lock the door?" he asked.

She smiled helplessly and ran a hand through her hair. She shrugged. "Does it matter?" she said and turned away.

He locked the door and followed her down the walk. She turned as he came up to her.

"It's a nice house," she murmured.

"Don't think about it," he said.

They turned their backs on their home and got in the ground car.

"Did you lock it?" asked the neighbor.

"Yes."

The neighbor smiled wryly. "So did we," he said. "I tried not to, but then I had to go back."

They moved through the quiet streets. The edges of the sky were beginning to redden. The neighbor's wife and the four children were in back. His wife and the neighbor were in front with him.

"Going to be a nice day," said the neighbor.

"I suppose so," he said.

"Have you told your children?" the neighbor asked softly.

"Of course not."

"I haven't, I haven't," insisted his neighbor, "I was just asking."

"Oh."

They rode in silence a while.

"Do you ever get the feeling that we're . . . running out?" asked the neighbor.

He tightened. "No," he said. His lips pressed together. "No."

"I guess it's better not to talk about it," his neighbor said hastily.

"Much better," he said.

As they drove up to the guardhouse at the gate, he turned to the back.

"Remember," he said. "Not a word from any of you."

The guard was sleepy and didn't care. The guard recognized him right away as the chief test pilot for the new ship. That was enough. The family was coming down to watch him off, he told the guard. That was all right. The guard let them drive to the ship's platform.

The car stopped under the huge columns. They all got out and stared up.

Far above them, its nose pointed toward the sky, the great metal ship was beginning to reflect the early morning glow.

"Let's go," he said. "Quickly."

As they hurried toward the ship's elevator, he stopped for a moment to look back. The guardhouse looked deserted. He looked around at everything and tried to fix it all in his memory.

He bent over and picked up some dirt. He put it in his pocket.

"Good-bye," he whispered.

He ran to the elevator.

The doors shut in front of them. There was no sound in the rising cubicle but the hum of the motor and a few self-conscious coughs from the children. He looked at them. To be taken so young, he thought, without a chance to help.

He closed his eyes. His wife's arm rested on his arm. He looked at her. Their eyes met and she smiled at him.

"It's all right," she whispered.

The elevator shuddered to a stop. The doors slid open and they went out. It was getting lighter. He hurried them along the enclosed platform.

They all climbed through the narrow doorway in the ship's side. He hesitated before following them. He wanted to say something fitting the moment. It burned in him to say something fitting the moment.

He couldn't. He swung in and grunted, as he pulled the door shut and turned the wheel tight.

"That's it," he said. "Come on, everybody."

Their footsteps echoed on the metal decks and ladders as they went up to the control room.

The children ran to the ports and looked out. They gasped when they saw how high they were. Their mothers stood behind them, looking down at the ground with frightened eyes.

He went up to them.

"So high," said his daughter.

He patted her head gently. "So high," he repeated.

Then he turned abruptly and went over to the instrument panel. He stood there hesitantly. He heard someone come up behind him.

"Shouldn't we tell the children?" asked his wife. "Shouldn't we let them know it's their last look?"

"Go ahead," he said. "Tell them."

He waited to hear her footsteps. There were none. He turned. She kissed him on the cheek. Then she went to tell the children.

He threw over the switch. Deep in the belly of the ship, a spark ignited the fuel. A concentrated rush of gas flooded from the vents. The bulkheads began to shake.

He heard his daughter crying. He tried not to listen. He extended a trembling hand toward the lever, then glanced back suddenly. They were all staring at him. He put his hand on the lever and threw it over.

The ship quivered a brief second and then they

felt it rush along the smooth incline. It flashed up into the air, faster and faster. They all heard the wind rushing past.

He watched the children turn to the ports and look out again.

"Good-bye," they said. "Good-bye."

He sank down wearily at the control panel. Out of the corner of his eyes he saw his neighbor sit down next to him.

"You know just where we're going?" his neighbor asked.

"On that chart there."

His neighbor looked at the chart. His eyebrows raised.

"In another solar system," he said.

"That's right. It has an atmosphere like ours. We'll be safe there."

"The race will be safe," said his neighbor.

He nodded once and looked back at his and his neighbor's family. They were still looking out the ports.

"What?" he asked.

"I said," the neighbor repeated, "which one of these planets is it?"

He leaned over the chart, pointed.

"That small one over there," he said. "Near that moon."

"This one, third from the sun?"

"That's right," he said. "That one. Third from the sun."

Keyhole

by Murray Leinster

WHEN THEY BROUGHT Butch into the station in Tycho Center he seemed to shrivel as the gravity coils in the air lock went on. To begin with, he was impossible. He was all big eyes and skinny arms and legs, and he was very young and he didn't need air to breathe. Worden saw him as a limp bundle of bristly fur and terrified eyes as his captors handed him over.

"Are you crazy?" demanded Worden angrily. "Bringing him in like this? Would you take a human baby into eight gravities? Get out of the way."

He rushed for the nursery that had been made ready for somebody like Butch. There was a re-built dwelling cave on one side. The other side was a schoolroom for humans. And under the

147

nursery the gravity coils had been turned off so
that in that room things had only the weight that
was proper to them on the Moon.

The rest of the station had coils to bring everything up to normal weight for Earth. Otherwise
the staff of the station would be seasick most of
the time. Butch was in the Earth gravity part of
the station when he was delivered, and he
couldn't lift a furry spindly paw.

In the nursery, though, it was different. Worden
put him on the floor. Worden was the uncomfortable one there — his weight only twenty
pounds instead of a normal hundred and sixty.
He swayed and reeled as a man does on the
Moon without gravity coils to steady him.

But that was the normal thing to Butch. He
uncurled himself and suddenly flashed across the
nursery to the reconstructed dwelling cave. It
was a pretty good job, that cave. There were the
five-foot chipped rocks shaped like dunce caps,
found in all residences of Butch's race. There
was the rocking stone on its base of other flat-
tened rocks. But the separate stones were fastened down with wire in case Butch got ideas.

Butch streaked it to these familiar objects. He
swarmed up one of the dunce-cap stones and
locked his arms and legs about its top, clinging
close. Then he was still. Worden regarded him.
Butch was motionless for minutes, seeming to

take in as much as possible of his surroundings without moving even his eyes.

Suddenly his head moved. He took in more of his environment. Then he stirred a third time and seemed to look at Worden with an extraordinary intensity — whether of fear or pleading Worden could not tell.

"Hmm," said Worden, "so that's what those stones are for! Perches or beds or roosts, eh? I'm your nurse, fella. We're playing a dirty trick on you, but we can't help it."

He knew Butch couldn't understand, but he talked to him as a man does talk to a dog or a baby. It isn't sensible, but it's necessary.

"We're going to raise you up to be a traitor to your kinfolk," he said with some grimness. "I don't like it, but it has to be done. So I'm going to be very kind to you as part of the conspiracy. Real kindness would suggest that I kill you instead — but I can't do that."

Butch stared at him, unblinking and motionless. He looked something like an Earth monkey but not too much so. He was completely impossible but he looked pathetic.

Worden said bitterly, "You're in your nursery, Butch. Make yourself at home!"

He went out and closed the door behind him. Outside he glanced at the video screens that showed the interior of the nursery from four different angles. Butch remained still for a long time. Then he slipped down to the floor. This time he ignored the dwelling cave of the nursery.

He went interestedly to the human culture part. He examined everything there with his oversized soft eyes. He touched everything with his incredibly handlike tiny paws. But his touches were tentative. Nothing was actually disturbed when he finished his examination.

He went swiftly back to the dunce-cap rock, swarmed up it, locked his arms and legs about it again, blinked rapidly and seemed to go to sleep. He remained motionless with closed eyes until Worden grew tired of watching him and moved away.

The whole affair was preposterous and infuriating. The first men to land on the Moon knew that it was a dead world. The astronomers had been saying so for a hundred years, and the first and second expeditions to reach Luna from Earth found nothing to contradict the theory.

But a man from the third expedition saw something moving up on the upflung rocks of the Moon's landscape and he shot it, and the existence of Butch's kind was discovered. It was inconceivable of course that there should be living creatures where there was neither air nor water. But Butch's folk did live under exactly those conditions.

The dead body of the first living creature killed on the Moon was carried back to Earth

and the biologists grew indignant. Even with a
specimen to dissect and study they were inclined
to insist that there simply wasn't any such creature. So the fourth and fifth and sixth lunar expeditions hunted Butch's relatives very earnestly for
further specimens for the advancement of science.

The sixth expedition lost two men whose space
suits were punctured by what seemed to be
weapons while they were hunting. The seventh
expedition was wiped out to the last man. Butch's
relatives evidently didn't like being shot as bi-
ological specimens.

It wasn't until the tenth expedition of four
ships established a base in Tycho Crater that men
had any assurance of being able to land on the
Moon and get away again. Even then the staff
of the station felt as if it were under permanent
siege.

Worden made his report to Earth. A baby lunar
creature had been captured by a tractor party
and brought into Tycho Station. A nursery was
ready and the infant was there now, alive. He
seemed to be uninjured. He seemed not to mind
an environment of breathable air for which he
had no use. He was active and apparently curious
and his intelligence was marked.

There was so far no clue to what he ate — if he
ate at all — though he had a mouth like the other
collected specimens and the toothlike concre-

tions which might serve as teeth. Worden would of course continue to report in detail. At the moment he was allowing Butch to accustom himself to his new surroundings.

He settled down in the recreation room to scowl at his companion scientists and try to think, despite the program beamed on radar frequency from Earth. He definitely didn't like his job, but he knew that it had to be done. Butch had to be domesticated. He had to be persuaded that he was a human being, so human beings could find out how to exterminate his kind.

It had been observed before, on Earth, that a kitten raised with a litter of puppies came to consider itself a dog and that even pet ducks came to prefer human society to that of their own species. Some talking birds of high intelligence appeared to be convinced that they were people and acted that way. If Butch reacted similarly he would become a traitor to his kind for the benefit of man. And it was necessary!

Men had to have the Moon, and that was all there was to it. Gravity on the Moon was one eighth that of gravity on Earth. A rocket ship could make the Moon voyage and carry a cargo, but no ship yet built could carry fuel for a trip to Mars or Venus if it started out from Earth.

With a fueling stop on the Moon, though, the matter was simple. Eight drums of rocket fuel on the Moon weighed no more than one on Earth.

A ship itself weighed only one eighth as much on Luna. So a rocket that took off from Earth with ten drums of fuel could stop at a fuel base on the Moon and soar away again with two hundred, and sometimes more.

With the Moon as a fueling base, men could conquer the solar system. Without the Moon, mankind was earthbound. Men had to have the Moon!

But Butch's relatives prevented it. By normal experience there could not be life on an airless desert with such monstrous extremes of heat and cold as the Moon's surface experienced. But there was life there. Butch's kinfolk did not breathe oxygen. Apparently they ate it in some mineral combination and it interacted with other minerals in their bodies to yield heat and energy.

Men thought squids peculiar because their blood stream used copper in place of iron, but Butch and his kindred seemed to have complex carbon compounds in place of both. They were intelligent in some fashion, it was clear. They used tools, they chipped stone, and they had long, needlelike stone crystals which they threw as weapons.

No metals, of course, for lack of fire to smelt them. There couldn't be fire without air. But Worden reflected that in ancient days some experimenters had melted metals and set wood ablaze with mirrors concentrating the heat of the sun. With the naked sunlight of the Moon's surface, not tempered by air and clouds, Butch's folk could have metals if they only contrived mirrors and curved them properly like the mirrors of telescopes on Earth.

Worden had an odd sensation just then. He looked around sharply as if somebody had made a sudden movement. But the video screen merely displayed a comedian back on Earth, wearing a funny hat. Everybody looked at the screen.

As Worden watched, the comedian was smothered in a mass of soapsuds and the studio audience two hundred and thirty thousand miles away squealed and applauded the exquisite humor of the scene. In the Moon station in Tycho Crater somehow it was less than comical.

Worden got up and shook himself. He went to look again at the screens that showed the interior of the nursery. Butch was motionless on the absurd cone-shaped stone. His eyes were closed. He was simply a furry, pathetic little bundle, stolen from the airless wastes outside to be bred into a traitor to his race.

Worden went to his cabin and turned in. Before he slept, though, he reflected that there was still some hope for Butch. Nobody understood his metabolism. Nobody could guess at what he ate. Butch might starve to death. If he did he would be lucky. But it was Worden's job to prevent it.

Butch's relatives were at war with men. The tractors that crashed away from the station — they went amazingly fast on the Moon—were watched by big-eyed furry creatures from rock crevices and from behind the boulders that dotted the lunar landscape.

Needle-sharp throwing stones flicked through emptiness. They splintered on the tractor bodies and on the tractor ports, but sometimes they jammed or broke a tread and then the tractor had to stop. Somebody had to go out and clear things or make repairs. And then a storm of throwing stones poured upon him.

A needle-pointed stone, traveling a hundred feet a second, hit just as hard on Luna as it did on Earth — and it traveled farther. Space suits were punctured. Men died. Now tractor treads were being armored and special repair suits were under construction, made of hardened steel plates.

Men who reached the Moon in rocket ships were having to wear armor like medieval knights and men-at-arms! There was a war on. A traitor was needed. And Butch was elected to be that traitor.

When Worden went into the nursery again — the days and nights on the Moon are two weeks long apiece, so men ignored such matters inside the station — Butch leaped for the dunce-cap stone and clung to its top. He had been fumbling around the rocking stone. It still swayed back and forth on its plate. Now he seemed to try to squeeze himself to unity with the stone spire, his eyes staring enigmatically at Worden.

"I don't know whether we'll get anywhere or not," said Worden conversationally. "Maybe you'll put up a fight if I touch you. But we'll see."

He reached out his hand. The small furry body — neither hot nor cold but the temperature of the air in the station — resisted desperately. But Butch was very young. Worden peeled him loose and carried him across the room to the human schoolroom equipment. Butch curled up, staring fearfully.

"I'm playing dirty," said Worden, "by being nice to you, Butch. Here's a toy."

Butch stirred in his grasp. His eyes blinked rapidly. Worden put him down and wound up a tiny mechanical toy. It moved. Butch watched intently. When it stopped he looked back at Worden. Worden wound it up again. Again Butch watched. When it ran down a second time the tiny handlike paw reached out.

With an odd tentativeness, Butch tried to turn the winding key. He was not strong enough. After an instant he went loping across to the dwelling cave. The winding key was a metal ring. Butch fitted that over a throw-stone point, and twisted the toy about. He wound it up. He put the toy on the floor and watched it work. Worden's jaw dropped.

"Brains!" he said wryly. "Too bad, Butch! You know the principle of the lever. At a guess, you're an eight-year-old human brain! I'm sorry for you, fella!"

At the regular communication hour he made his report to Earth. Butch was teachable. He only had to see a thing done once — or at most twice — to be able to repeat the motions involved.

"And," said Worden, carefully detached, "he isn't afraid of me now. He understands that I intend to be friendly. While I was carrying him I talked to him. He felt the vibrations of my chest from my voice.

"Just before I left him I picked him up and talked to him again. He looked at my mouth as it moved and put his paw on my chest to feel the vibrations. I put his paw at my throat. The vibrations are clearer there. He seemed fascinated. I don't know how you'd rate his intelligence, but it's above that of a human baby."

Then he said with even greater detachment, "I am disturbed. If you must know, I don't like the idea of exterminating his kind. They have tools, they have intelligence. I think we should try to communicate with them in some way — try to make friends — stop killing them for dissection."

The communicator was silent for the second and a half it took his voice to travel to Earth and the second and a half it took to come back. Then the recording clerk's voice said briskly, "Very good, Mr. Worden! Your voice was very clear."

Worden shrugged his shoulders. The lunar station in Tycho was a highly official enterprise. The staff on the Moon had to be competent — and besides, political appointees did not want to risk their precious lives — but the Earth end of the business of the Space Exploration Bureau was run by the sort of people who do get on official payrolls. Worden felt sorry for Butch — and for Butch's relatives.

In a later lesson session Worden took an empty coffee tin into the nursery. He showed Butch that its bottom vibrated when he spoke into it, just as his throat did. Butch experimented busily. He discovered for himself that it had to be pointed at Worden to catch the vibrations.

Worden was unhappy. He would have preferred Butch to be a little less rational. But for the next lesson he presented Butch with a really thin metal diaphragm stretched across a hoop. Butch caught the idea at once.

When Worden made his next report to Earth he felt angry. "Butch has no experience of sound as we have, of course," he said curtly. "There's no air on the Moon. But sound travels through rocks. He's sensitive to vibrations in solid objects, just as a deaf person can feel the vibrations of a dance floor if the music is loud enough.

"Maybe Butch's kind has a language or a code of sounds sent through the rock underfoot. They do communicate somehow! And if they've brains and a means of communication they aren't animals and shouldn't be exterminated for our convenience."

He stopped. The chief biologist of the Space Exploration Bureau was at the other end of the communication beam. Then after the necessary pause for distance his voice came blandly.

"Splendid, Worden! Splendid reasoning! But we have to take the longer view. Exploration of Mars and Venus is a very popular idea with the public. If we are to have funds — and the appropriations come up for a vote shortly — we have to make progress toward the nearer planets. The public demands it. Unless we can begin work on a refueling base on the Moon, public interest will cease!"

Worden said urgently, "Suppose I send some pictures of Butch? He's very human, sir! He's extraordinarily appealing! He has personality! A reel or two of Butch at his lessons ought to be popular!"

Again that irritating wait while his voice traveled a quarter-million miles at the speed of light and the wait for the reply.

"The — ah — lunar creatures. Worden," said the chief biologist regretfully, "have killed a number of men who have been publicized as martyrs to science. We cannot give favorable publicity to creatures that have killed men!" Then he added blandly, "But you are progressing splendidly, Worden, *splendidly!* Carry on!"

His image faded from the video screen. Worden said naughty words as he turned away. He'd come to like Butch. Butch trusted him. Butch now slid down from that crazy perch of his and came rushing to his arms every time he entered the nursery.

Butch was ridiculously small — no more than eighteen inches high. He was preposterously light and fragile in his nursery where only Moon gravity obtained. And Butch was such an earnest little creature, so soberly absorbed in everything that Worden showed him!

He was still fascinated by the phenomena of sound. Humming or singing — even Worden's humming and singing — entranced him. When Worden's lips moved now Butch struck an attitude and held up the hoop with a tiny finger pressed to it to catch the vibrations Worden's voice and diaphragm made.

Now too when he grasped an idea Worden tried to convey, he tended to swagger. He became more human in his actions with every session of human contact. Once, indeed, Worden looked at the video screens which spied on Butch and saw him — all alone — solemnly going through every gesture and every movement Wor-

den had made. He was pretending to be Worden,
apparently for his own satisfaction!

Worden felt a lump in his throat. He was enormously fond of the little mite. It was painful that
he had just left Butch to help in the construction
of a vibrator-microphone device which would
transfer his voice to rock vibrations, and simultaneously pick up any other vibrations that might
be made in return.

If the members of Butch's race did communicate by tapping on rocks or the like, men could
eavesdrop on them — could locate them, could
detect ambushes in preparation — and apply mankind's deadly military countermeasures.

Worden hoped the gadget wouldn't work. But
it did. When he put it on the floor of the nursery
and spoke into the microphone, Butch did feel
the vibrations underfoot. He recognized their
identity with the vibrations he'd learned to detect in air.

He made a skipping exultant hop and jump. It
was plainly the uttermost expression of satisfaction. And then his tiny foot pattered and
scratched furiously on the floor. It made a peculiar scratchy tapping noise which the microphone
picked up. Butch watched Worden's face, making
the sounds which were like highly elaborate foot-
falls.

"No dice, Butch," said Worden unhappily. "I
can't understand it. But it looks as if you've

started your treason already. This'll help wipe out some of your folks."

He reported it reluctantly to the head of the station. Microphones were immediately set into the rocky crater floor outside the station, and others were made ready for exploring parties to use for the detection of Moon creatures near them. Oddly enough, the microphones by the station yielded results right away.

It was near sunset. Butch had been captured near the middle of the three-hundred-and-thirty-four-hour lunar day. In all the hours between — a week by Earth time — he had had no nourishment of any sort. Worden had conscientiously offered him every edible and inedible substance in the Station collection.

Butch regarded them all with interest but without appetite. Worden — liking Butch — expected him to die of starvation and thought it a good idea. Better than encompassing the death of all his race, anyhow. And it did seem to him that Butch was beginning to show a certain sluggishness, a certain lack of bounce and energy. He thought it was weakness from hunger.

Sunset progressed. Yard by yard, fathom by fathom, half mile by half mile, the shadows of the miles-high western walls of Tycho crept across the crater floor. There came a time when only the central hump had sunlight. Then the shadow began to creep up the eastern walls. Presently the last thin jagged line of light would vanish and the colossal cup of the crater would be filled to overflowing with the night.

Worden watched the incandescent sunlight growing even narrower on the cliffs. He would see no other sunlight for two weeks' Earth time. Then abruptly an alarm bell rang. It clanged stridently, furiously. Doors hissed shut dividing the station into airtight sections.

Loud-speakers snapped. *"Noises in the rock outside! Sounds like Moon creatures talking nearby! They may plan an attack! Everybody into space suits and get guns ready!"*

At just that instant the last thin sliver of sunshine disappeared. Worden thought instantly of Butch. There was no space suit to fit him. Then he grimaced a little. Butch didn't need a space suit.

Worden got into the clumsy outfit. The lights dimmed. The harsh airless space outside the station was suddenly bathed in light. The multimillion-lumen beam, made to guide rocket ships to a landing even at night, was turned on to expose any creatures with designs on its owners. It was startling to see how little space was really lighted by the beam and how much of stark blackness spread on beyond.

The loud-speaker snapped again, *"Two Moon creatures! Running away! They're zigzagging! Anybody who wants to take a shot —"* The voice paused. It didn't matter. Nobody is a crack shot in a spacesuit. "They've left something behind," said the voice in the loud-speaker. It was sharp and uneasy.

"I'll take a look at that," said Worden. His own voice startled him, but he was depressed. "I've got a hunch what it is."

Minutes later he went through the air lock. He moved lightly despite the cumbrous suit he wore. There were two other staff members with him. All three were armed and the searchlight beam stabbed here and there erratically to expose any relative of Butch who might try to approach them in the darkness.

With the light at his back Worden could see that trillions of stars looked down upon Luna. The zenith was filled with infinitesimal specks of light of every conceivable color. The familiar constellations burned ten times as brightly as on Earth. And Earth itself hung nearly overhead. It was three quarters full — a monstrous bluish giant in the sky, four times the Moon's diameter, its icecaps and continents mistily to be seen.

Worden went forebodingly to the object left behind by Butch's kin. He wasn't much surprised when he saw what it was. It was a rocking stone on its plate with a fine impalpable dust on the plate, as if something had been crushed under the egg-shaped upper stone acting as a mill.

Worden said sourly into his helmet microphone,

"It's a present for Butch. His kinfolk know he was captured alive. They suspect he's hungry. They've left some grub for him of the kind he wants or needs most."

That was plainly what it was. It did not make Worden feel proud. A baby — Butch — had been kidnaped by the enemies of its race. That baby was a prisoner and its captors would have nothing with which to feed it. So someone, greatly daring — Worden wondered somberly if it was Butch's father and mother — had risked their lives to leave food for him with a rocking stone to tag it for recognition as food.

"It's a dirty shame," said Worden bitterly. "All right! Let's carry it back. Careful not to spill the powdered stuff!"

His lack of pride was emphasized when Butch fell upon the unidentified powder with marked enthusiasm. Tiny pinch by tiny pinch Butch consumed it with an air of vast satisfaction. Worden felt ashamed.

"You're getting treated pretty rough, Butch," said Worden. "What I've already learned from you will cost a good many hundreds of your folks' lives. And they're taking chances to feed you! I'm making you a traitor and myself a scoundrel."

Butch thoughtfully held up the hoop diaphragm to catch the voice vibrations in the air. He was small and furry and absorbed. He decided that he could pick up sounds better from the rock underfoot. He pressed the communicator microphone on Worden. He waited.

"No!" said Worden roughly. "Your people are too human. Don't let me find out any more, Butch. Be smart and play dumb!"

But Butch didn't. It wasn't very long before Worden was teaching him to read. Oddly, though, the rock microphones that had given the alarm at the station didn't help the tractor parties at all. Butch's kinfolk seemed to vanish from the neighborhood of the station altogether. Of course if that kept up, the construction of a fuel base could be begun and the actual extermination of the species carried out later. But the reports on Butch were suggesting other possibilities.

"If your folks stay vanished," Worden told Butch, "it'll be all right for a while — but only for a while. I'm being urged to try to get you used to Earth gravity. If I succeed, they'll want you on Earth in a zoo. And if that works — why, they'll be sending other expeditions to get more of your kinfolk to put in other zoos."

Butch watched Worden, motionless.

"And also" — Worden's tone was very grim — "there's some miniature mining machinery coming up by the next rocket. I'm supposed to see if you can learn to run it."

Butch made scratching sounds on the floor. It was unintelligible of course, but it was an expression of interest at least. Butch seemed to enjoy the vibrations of Worden's voice, just as a dog likes to have his master talk to him. Worden grunted.

"We humans class you as an animal, Butch. We tell ourselves that all the animal world should be subject to us. Animals should work for us. If you act too smart, we'll hunt down all your relatives and set them to work digging minerals for us. You'll be with them. But I don't want you to work your heart out in a mine, Butch! It's wrong!"

Butch remained quite still. Worden thought sickly of small furry creatures like Butch driven to labor in airless mines in the Moon's depths. With guards in space suits watching lest any try to escape to the freedom they'd known before the coming of men. With guns mounted against revolt. With punishments for rebellion or weariness.

It wouldn't be unprecedented. The Indians in Cuba when the Spanish came . . . Negro slavery in both Americas . . . concentration camps. . . .

Butch moved. He put a small furry paw on Worden's knee. Worden scowled at him.

"Bad business," he said harshly. "I'd rather not get fond of you. You're a likable little cuss, but your race is doomed. The trouble is that you didn't bother to develop a civilization. And if you had, I suspect we'd have smashed it. We humans aren't what you'd call admirable."

Butch went over to the blackboard. He took a

piece of pastel chalk — ordinary chalk was too hard for his Moon gravity muscles to use — and soberly began to make marks on the slate. The marks formed letters. The letters made words. The words made sense.

YOU, wrote Butch quite incredibly in neat pica lettering, GOOD FRIEND.

He turned his head to stare at Worden. Worden went white. "I haven't taught you those words, Butch!" he said very quietly. "What's up?"

He'd forgotten that his words to Butch were merely vibrations in the air or in the floor. He'd forgotten they had no meaning. But Butch seemed to have forgotten it too. He marked soberly:

MY FRIEND GET SPACE SUIT. He looked at Worden and marked once more. TAKE ME OUT. I COME BACK WITH YOU.

He looked at Worden with large incongruously soft and appealing eyes. And Worden's brain seemed to spin inside his skull. After a long time Butch printed again — YES.

Then Worden sat very still indeed. There was only Moon gravity in the nursery and he weighed only one eighth as much as on Earth. But he felt very weak. Then he felt grim.

"Not much else to do, I suppose," he said slowly. "But I'll have to carry you through Earth gravity to the air lock."

He got to his feet. Butch made a little leap up

into his arms. He curled up there, staring at Worden's face. Just before Worden stepped through the door, Butch reached up a skinny paw and caressed Worden's cheek tentatively.

"Here we go!" said Worden. "The idea was for you to be a traitor. I wonder — "

But with Butch a furry ball, suffering in the multiplied weight Earth gravity imposed upon him, Worden made his way to the air lock. He donned a spacesuit. He went out.

It was near sunrise then. A long time had passed and Earth was now in its last quarter and the very highest peak of all that made up the crater wall glowed incandescent in the sunshine. But the stars were still quite visible and very bright. Worden walked away from the station, guided by the Earth-shine on the ground underfoot.

Three hours later he came back. Butch skipped and hopped beside the space-suited figure. Behind them came two other figures. They were smaller than Worden but much larger than Butch. They were skinny and furry and they carried a burden. A mile from the station he switched on his suit radio. He called. A startled voice answered in his earphones.

"It's Worden," he said dryly. "I've been out for a walk with Butch. We visited his family and I've a couple of his cousins with me. They want to pay a visit and present some gifts. Will you let us in without shooting?"

There were exclamations. There was confusion. But Worden went on steadily toward the station while another high peak glowed in sunrise light, and a third seemed to burst into candescence. Dawn was definitely on the way.

The air-lock door opened. The party from the airless Moon went in. When the air lock filled, though, and the gravity coils went on, Butch and his relatives became helpless. They had to be carried to the nursery. There they uncurled themselves and blinked enigmatically at the men who crowded into the room where gravity was normal for the Moon and at the other men who stared in the door.

"I've got a sort of message," said Worden. "Butch and his relatives want to make a deal with us. You'll notice that they've put themselves at our mercy. We can kill all three of them. But they want to make a deal."

The head of the station said uncomfortably, "You've managed two-way communication, Worden?"

"I haven't," Worden told him. "They have. They've proved to me that they've brains equal to ours. They've been treated as animals and shot as specimens. They've fought back — naturally! But they want to make friends. They say that we can never use the Moon except in space suits and in stations like this, and they could never take Earth's gravity. So there's no need for us to be enemies. We can help each other."

The head of the station said dryly. "Plausible enough, but we have to act under orders, Worden. Did you explain that?"

"They know," said Worden. "So they've got set to to defend themselves if necessary. They've set up smelters to handle metals. They get the heat by sun mirrors, concentrating sunlight. They've even begun to work with gases held in containers. They're not far along with electronics yet, but they've got the theoretic knowledge and they don't need vacuum tubes. They live in a vacuum. They can defend themselves from now on."

The head said mildly, "I've watched Butch, you know, Worden. And you don't look crazy. But if this sort of thing is sprung on the armed forces on Earth, there'll be trouble. They've been arguing for armed rocket ships. If your friends start a real war for defense — if they can — maybe rocket warships will be the answer."

Worden nodded.

"Right. But our rockets aren't so good that they can fight this far from a fuel store, and there couldn't be one on the Moon with all of Butch's kinfolk civilized — as they nearly are now and as they certainly will be within the next few weeks. Smart people, these cousins and such of Butch!"

"I'm afraid they'll have to prove it," said the head. "Where'd they get this sudden surge in culture?"

"From us," said Worden. "Smelting from me, I think. Metallurgy and mechanical engineering from the tractor mechanics. Geology — call it lunology here — mostly from you."

"How's that?" demanded the head.

"Think of something you'd like Butch to do," said Worden grimly, "and then watch him."

The head stared and then looked at Butch — small and furry and swaggering. Butch stood up and bowed profoundly from the waist. One paw was placed where his heart could be. The other made a grandiose sweeping gesture. He straightened up and strutted, then climbed swiftly into Worden's lap and put a skinny furry arm about his neck.

"That bow," said the head, very pale, "is what I had in mind. You mean — "

"Just so," said Worden. "Butch's ancestors had no air to make noises in nor speech. So they developed telepathy. In time, to be sure, they worked out something like music — sounds carried through rock. But, like our music, it doesn't carry meaning. They communicated directly from mind to mind. Only we can't pick up communications from them, and they can from us."

"They read our minds!" said the head. He licked his lips. "And when we first shot them for specimens they were trying to communicate. Now they fight."

"Naturally," said Worden. "Wouldn't we? They've been picking our brains. They can put up a terrific battle now. They could wipe out this station without trouble. They let us stay so they could learn from us. Now they want to trade."

"We have to report to Earth," said the head slowly, "but — "

"They brought along some samples," said Worden. "They'll swap diamonds, weight for weight, for records. They like our music. They'll trade emeralds for textbooks — they can read now! And they'll set up an atomic pile and swap plutonium for other things they'll think of later. Trading on that basis should be cheaper than a war!"

"Yes," said the head. "It should. That's the sort of argument men will listen to. But how — "

"Butch," said Worden ironically. "Just Butch! We didn't capture him — they planted him on us! He stayed in the station and picked our brains and relayed the stuff to his relatives. We wanted to learn about them, remember? It's like the story of the psychologist . . ."

History Lesson

by Arthur C. Clarke

No one could remember when the tribe had begun its long journey. The land of great rolling plains that had been its first home was now no more than a half-forgotten dream.

For many years Shann and his people had been fleeing through a country of low hills and sparkling lakes, and now the mountains lay ahead. This summer they must cross them to the southern lands. There was little time to lose. The white terror which had come down from the Poles, grinding continents to dust and freezing the very air before it, was less than a day's march behind.

Shann wondered if the glaciers could climb the mountains ahead, and within his heart he dared to kindle a little flame of hope. This might prove a barrier against which even the remorseless ice would batter in vain. In the southern lands of which the legends spoke, his people might find refuge at last.

It took weeks to discover a pass through which the tribe and the animals could travel. When midsummer came, they had camped in a lonely valley where the air was thin and the stars shone with a brilliance no one had ever seen before.

The summer was waning when Shann took his two sons and went ahead to explore the way. For three days they climbed, and for three nights slept as best they could on the freezing rocks, and on the fourth morning there was nothing ahead but a gentle rise to a cairn of gray stones built by other travelers centuries ago.

Shann felt himself trembling, and not with cold, as they walked toward the little pyramid of stones. His sons had fallen behind. No one spoke, for too much was at stake. In a little while they could know if all their hopes had been betrayed.

To east and west, the wall of mountains curved away as if embracing the land beneath. Below lay endless miles of undulating plain, with a great river swinging across it in tremendous loops. It was a fertile land, one in which the tribe could raise crops knowing that there would be no need to flee before the harvest came.

Then Shann lifted his eyes to the south, and saw the doom of all his hopes. For there at the edge of the world glimmered that deadly light he had seen so often to the north — the glint of ice below the horizon.

There was no way forward. Through all the years of flight, the glaciers from the south had been advancing to meet them. Soon they would be crushed beneath the moving walls of ice. . . .

Southern glaciers did not reach the mountains until a generation later. In that last summer the sons of Shann carried the sacred treasures of the tribe to the lonely cairn overlooking the plain. The ice that had once gleamed below the horizon was now almost at their feet. By spring it would be splintering against the mountain walls.

No one understood the treasures now. They were from a past too distant for the understanding of any man alive. Their origins were lost in the mists that surrounded the Golden Age, and how they had come at last into the possession of this wandering tribe was a story that now would never be told. For it was the story of a civilization that had passed beyond recall.

Once, all these pitiful relics had been treasured for some good reason, and now they had become sacred though their meaning had long been lost. The print in the old books had faded centuries ago though much of the lettering was still visible — if there had been any to read it. But many generations had passed since anyone had had a use for a set of seven-figure logarithms, an atlas of the world, and the score of Sibelius' Seventh Symphony printed, according to the flyleaf, by H.K. Chu and Sons, at the City of Peking in the year A.D. 2371.

The old books were placed reverently in the little crypt that had been made to receive them. There followed a motley collection of fragments — gold and platinum coins, a broken telephoto lens, a watch, a cold-light lamp, a microphone, the cutter from an electric razor, some midget radio tubes, the flotsam that had been left behind when the great tide of civilization had ebbed forever.

All these treasures were carefully stowed away in their resting place. Then came three more relics, the most sacred of all because the least understood.

The first was a strangely shaped piece of metal, showing the coloration of the intense heat. It was, in its way, the most pathetic of all these symbols from the past, for it told of man's greatest achievement and of the future he might have known. The mahogany stand on which it was mounted bore a silver plate with the inscription:

Auxiliary Igniter from Starboard Jet
Spaceship *Morning Star*
Earth-Moon, A.D. 1985

Next followed another miracle of the ancient

science — a sphere of transparent plastic with strangely shaped pieces of metal embedded in it. At its center was a tiny capsule of synthetic radio-element, surrounded by the converging screens that shifted its radiation far down the spectrum. As long as the materials remained active, the sphere would be a tiny radio transmitter, broadcasting power in all directions. Only a few of these spheres had ever been made. They had been designed as perpetual beacons to mark the orbits of the asteroids. But man had never reached the asteroids and the beacons had never been used.

Last of all was a flat, circular tin, wide in comparison with its depth. It was heavily sealed, and rattled when shaken. The tribal lore predicted that disaster would follow if it was ever opened, and no one knew that it held one of the great works of art of nearly a thousand years before.

The work was finished. The two men rolled the stones back into place and slowly began to descend the mountainside. Even to the last, man had given some thought to the future and had tried to preserve something for posterity.

That winter the great waves of ice began their first assault on the mountain, attacking from north and south. The foothills were overwhelmed in the first onslaught, and the glaciers ground them into dust. But the mountains stood firm, and when the summer came the ice retreated for a while.

So, winter after winter, the battle continued, and the roar of the avalanches, the grinding of rock, and the explosions of splintering ice filled the air with tumult. No war of man's had been fiercer than this, and even man's battles had not quite engulfed the globe as this had done.

At last the tidal waves of ice began to subside and to creep slowly down the flanks of the mountains they had never quite subdued. The valleys and passes were still firmly in their grip. It was stalemate. The glaciers had met their match, but their defeat was too late to be of any use to man.

So the centuries passed, and presently there happened something that must occur once at least in the history of every world in the universe, no matter how remote and lonely it may be.

The ship from Venus came five thousand years too late, but its crew knew nothing of this. While still many millions of miles away, the telescopes had seen the great shroud of ice that made Earth the most brilliant object in the sky next to the sun itself.

Here and there the dazzling sheet was marred by black specks that revealed the presence of almost buried mountains. That was all. The rolling oceans, the plains and forests, the deserts and lakes — all that had been the world of man — was sealed beneath the ice, perhaps forever.

The ship closed in to Earth and established an

orbit less than a thousand miles away. For five days it circled the planet while cameras recorded all that was left to see and a hundred instruments gathered information that would give the Venusian scientists many years of work.

An actual landing was not intended. There seemed little purpose in it. But on the sixth day the picture changed. A panoramic monitor, driven to the limit of its amplification, detected the dying radiation of the five-thousand-year-old beacon. Through all the centuries, it had been sending out its signals with ever-failing strength as its radioactive heart steadily weakened.

The monitor locked on the beacon frequency. In the control room, a bell clamored for attention. A little later, the Venusian ship broke free from its orbit and slanted down toward Earth, toward a range of mountains that still towered proudly above the ice, and to a cairn of gray stones that the years had scarcely touched. . . .

The great disk of the sun blazed fiercely in a sky no longer veiled with mist, for the clouds that had once hidden Venus had now completely gone. Whatever force had caused the change in the sun's radiation had doomed one civilization, but had given birth to another. Less than five thousand years before, the half-savage people of Venus had seen sun and stars for the first time. Just as the science of Earth had begun with astronomy,

so had that of Venus, and on the warm, rich
world that man had never seen, progress had been
incredibly rapid.

Perhaps the Venusians had been lucky. They
never knew the Dark Ages that held man en-
chained for a thousand years. They missed the
long detour into chemistry and mechanics but
came at once to the more fundamental laws of
radiation physics. In the time that man had taken
to progress from the pyramids to the rocket-
propelled spaceship, the Venusians had passed
from the discovery of agriculture to antigravity
itself — the ultimate secret that man had never
learned.

The warm ocean that still bore most of the
young planet's life rolled its breakers languidly
against the sandy shore. So new was this continent
that the very sands were coarse and gritty. There
had not yet been time enough for the sea to wear
them smooth.

The scientists lay half in the water, their beautiful reptilian bodies gleaming in the sunlight.
The greatest minds of Venus had gathered on
this shore from all the islands of the planet. What
they were going to hear they did not know, except
that it concerned the Third World and the mysterious race that had peopled it before the coming
of ice.

The Historian was standing on the land, for
the instruments he wished to use had no love of

water. By his side was a large machine which attracted many curious glances from his colleagues. It was clearly concerned with optics, for a lens system projected from it toward a screen of white material a dozen yards away.

The Historian began to speak. Briefly he recapitulated what little had been discovered concerning the Third Planet and its people.

He mentioned the centuries of fruitless research that had failed to interpret a single word of the writings of Earth. The planet had been inhabited by a race of great technical ability. That, at least, was proved by the few pieces of machinery that had been found in the cairn upon the mountain.

"We do not know why so advanced a civilization came to an end," he observed. "Almost certainly, it had sufficient knowledge to survive an Ice Age. Possibly disease or racial degeneration may have been responsible. There must have been some other factor of which we know nothing. It has even been suggested that the tribal conflicts endemic to our own species in prehistoric times may have continued on the Third Planet after the coming of technology.

"Some philosophers maintain that knowledge of machinery does not necessarily imply a high degree of civilization, and it is theoretically possible to have wars in a society possessing mechanical power, flight, and even radio. Such a conception is alien to our thoughts, but we must admit its possibility. It would certainly account for the downfall of the lost race.

"It has always been assumed that we should never know anything of the physical form of the creatures who lived on Planet Three. For centuries our artists have been depicting scenes from the history of the dead world, peopling it with all manner of fantastic beings. Most of these creations have resembled us more or less closely, though it has often been pointed out that because we are reptiles it does not follow that all intelligent life must necessarily be reptilian.

"We now know the answer to one of the most baffling problems of history. At last, after hundreds of years of research, we have discovered the exact form and nature of the ruling life on the Third Planet."

There was a murmur of astonishment from the assembled scientists. Some were so taken aback that they disappeared for a while into the comfort of the ocean, as all Venusians were apt to do in moments of stress. The Historian waited until his colleagues reemerged into the element they so disliked. He himself was quite comfortable, thanks to the tiny sprays that were continually playing over his body. With their help he could live on land for many hours before having to return to the ocean.

The excitement slowly subsided and the lecturer continued:

"One of the most puzzling of the objects found on Planet Three was a flat metal container holding a great length of transparent plastic material, perforated at the edges and wound tightly into a spool. This transparent tape at first seemed quite featureless, but an examination with the new subelectronic microscope has shown that this is not the case. Along the surface of the material, invisible to our eyes but perfectly clear under the correct radiation, are literally thousands of tiny pictures. It is believed that they were imprinted on the material by some chemical means, and have faded with the passage of time.

"These pictures apparently form a record of life as it was on the Third Planet at the height of its civilization. They are not independent. Consecutive pictures are almost identical, differing only in the detail of movement. The purpose of such a record is obvious. It is only necessary to project the scenes in rapid succession to give an illusion of continuous movement. We have made a machine to do this and I have here an exact reproduction of the picture sequence.

"The scenes you are now going to witness take us back many thousands of years to the great days of our sister planet. They show a complex civilization, many of whose activities we can only dimly understand. Life seems to have been very

violent and energetic, and much that you will see
is quite baffling.

"It is clear that the Third Planet was inhabited
by a number of different species, none of them
reptilian. That is a blow to our pride, but the
conclusion is inescapable. The dominant type of
life appears to have been a two-armed biped. It
walked upright and covered its body with some
flexible material, possibly for protection against
the cold, since even before the Ice Age the planet
was at a much lower temperature than our own
world. But I will not try your patience any
longer. You will now see the record of which I
have been speaking."

A brilliant light flashed from the projector.
There was a gentle whirring and on the screen
appeared hundreds of strange beings moving
rather jerkily to and fro. The picture expanded
to embrace one of the creatures, and the scientists could see that the Historian's description
had been correct.

The creature possessed two eyes, set rather
close together, but the other facial adornments
were a little obscure. There was a large orifice
in the lower portion of the head that was continually opening and closing. Possibly it had something to do with the creature's breathing.

The scientists watched spellbound as the strange
being became involved in a series of fantastic
adventures. There was an incredibly violent con-

flict with another, slightly different creature. It seemed certain that they must both be killed, but when it was all over neither seemed any the worse.

Then came a furious drive over miles of country in a four-wheeled mechanical device which was capable of extraordinary feats of locomotion. The ride ended in a city packed with other vehicles moving in all directions at breathtaking speeds. No one was surprised to see two of the machines meet head-on with devastating results.

After that, events became even more complicated. It was now quite obvious that it would take many years of research to analyze and understand all that was happening. It was also clear that the record was a work of art, somewhat stylized, rather than an exact reproduction of life as it actually had been on the Third Planet.

Most of the scientists felt themselves completely dazed when the sequence of pictures came to an end. There was a final flurry of motion in which the creature that had been the center of interest became involved in some tremendous, but incomprehensible catastrophe. The picture contracted to a circle, centered on the creature's head.

The last scene of all was an expanded view of its face, obviously expressing some powerful emotion. But whether it was rage, grief, defiance, resignation, or some other feeling could not be guessed. The picture vanished. For a moment some lettering appeared on the screen, then it was all over.

For several minutes there was a complete silence, save for the lapping of the waves upon the sand. The scientists were too stunned to speak. The fleeting glimpse of Earth's civilization had had a shattering effect on their minds. Then little groups began to start talking together, first in whispers and then more and more loudly as the implications of what they had seen became clearer. Presently the Historian called for attention and addressed the meeting again.

"We are now planning," he said, "a vast program of research to extract all available knowledge from this record. Thousands of copies are being made for distribution to all workers. You will appreciate the problems involved. The psychologists in particular have an immense task confronting them.

"But I do not doubt that we shall succeed. In another generation, who can say what we may not have learned of their wonderful race? Before we leave, let us look again at our remote cousins, whose wisdom may have surpassed our own but of whom so little has survived."

Once more the final picture flashed on the screen, motionless this time for the projector had been stopped. With something like awe, the scientists gazed at the still figure from the past, while in turn the little biped stared at them with its characteristic expression of arrogant bad temper.

For the rest of time it would symbolize the human race. The psychologists of Venus would analyze its actions and watch its every movement until they could reconstruct its mind. Thousands of books would be written about it. Intricate philosophies would be contrived to account for its behavior.

But all this labor, all this research, would be utterly in vain. Perhaps the proud and lonely figure on the screen was smiling sardonically at the scientists who were starting on their age-long fruitless quest.

Its secret would be safe as long as the universe endured, for no one now would ever read the lost language of Earth. Millions of times in the ages to come those last few words would flash across the screen and none could ever guess their meaning:

A Walt Disney Production.